YORK NOTES

ANIMAL FARM

PWN ORWELL

A OPALINSKA

Longman
is an imprint of

PEARSON

 York Press

YORK PRESS
322 Old Brompton Road, London SW5 9JH

PEARSON EDUCATION LIMITED
Edinburgh Gate, Harlow,
Essex CM20 2JE, United Kingdom
Associated companies, branches and representatives throughout the world

First published 1997
New edition 2002
This new and fully revised edition 2011

10 9 8 7 6 5 4

ISBN 978–1–4082–7002–8

Illustrated by John Dillow; and Neil Gower (p. 6)

Photographs of George Orwell, Joseph Stalin and Leon Trotsky reproduced by kind permission of Getty Images

Phototypeset by Border Consultants, Dorset

Printed in China (CTPS/04)

PART ONE: INTRODUCTION

Study and revision advice

There are two main stages to your reading and work on *Animal Farm*. First, the study of the novel as you read it. Second, your preparation or revision for the exam or controlled assessment. These top tips will help you with both.

 ### READING AND STUDYING THE BOOK – DEVELOP INDEPENDENCE!

- Try to engage and respond **personally** to the characters, ideas and story – not just for your enjoyment, but also because it helps you develop your own **independent ideas and thoughts** about the novel. This is something that examiners are very keen to see.
- **Talk** about the text with friends and family; ask questions in class; put forward your own viewpoint – and, if you have time, **read around** the text to find out about *Animal Farm*.
- Take time to **consider** and **reflect** on the **key elements** of the novel; keep your own notes, mind-maps, diagrams, scribbled jottings about the characters and how you respond to them; follow the story as it progresses (what do you think might happen?); discuss the main themes and ideas (what do *you* think it is about? Politics? Power? Education?); pick out language that impresses you or makes an **impact**, and so on.
- Treat your studying **creatively**. When you write essays or give talks about the novel make your responses creative. Think about using really clear ways of explaining yourself, use unusual **quotations** and well-chosen **vocabulary**, and try powerful, persuasive ways of beginning or ending what you say or write.

 ### REVISION – DEVELOP ROUTINES AND PLANS!

- **Good revision** comes from **good planning**. Find out when your exam or controlled assessment is and then plan to look at key aspects of *Animal Farm* on different days or at different times during your revision period. You could use these Notes – see **How can these Notes help me?** – and add dates or times when you are going to cover a particular topic.
- Use **different ways** of **revising**. Sometimes talking about the text and what you know/don't know with a friend or member of the family can help; at other times, using different colour pens to fill a sheet of A4 with all your ideas about a character, for example Boxer, can make ideas come alive; alternatively, making short lists of quotations to learn, or numbering events in the plot can assist you.
- **Practise plans** and **essays**. As you get nearer the 'day', start by looking at essay **questions** and writing short bulleted plans. Do several plans (you don't have to write the whole essay); then take those plans and add details to them (quotations, linked ideas). Finally, using the advice in **Part Six: Grade Booster**, write some practice essays and then check them out against the advice we have provided.

 **EXAMINER'S TIP**

Prepare for the exam/controlled assessment. Whatever you need to bring, make sure you have it with you – books (if you're allowed), pens, pencils – and make sure you turn up on time!

Introducing *Animal Farm*

SETTING

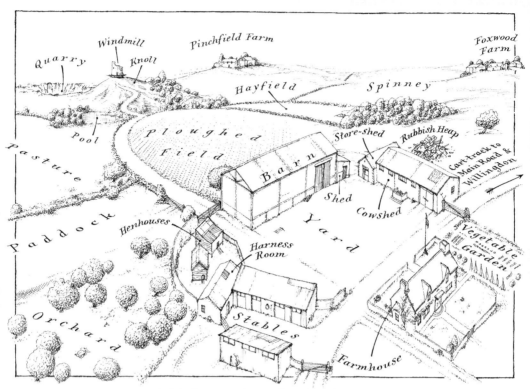

A bird's eye view of Animal Farm

CHARACTERS: WHO'S WHO

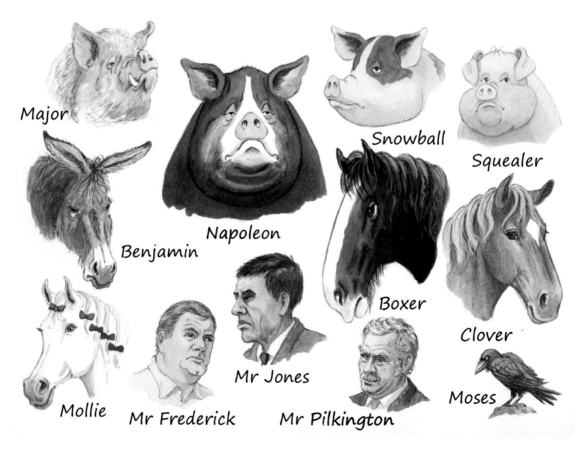

Major

Benjamin

Napoleon

Snowball

Squealer

Boxer

Clover

Mollie

Mr Frederick

Mr Jones

Mr Pilkington

Moses

GEORGE ORWELL: AUTHOR AND CONTEXT

1903	Eric Arthur Blair born 25 June, in Bengal, India; family soon returns to England
1936	Fights for the Republicans in the Spanish Civil War
1943	War correspondent for the *Observer*; leaves the BBC after two years; writes *Animal Farm*
1945	*Animal Farm* published
1947	Moves to the Hebridean island of Jura; health deteriorates further
1949	*Nineteen Eighty-Four* published
1950	Dies of tuberculosis on 21 January

HISTORICAL CONTEXT

Animal Farm is an allegory of historical events in Russia following the fall of the Tsar in 1917 and the seizing of power by the Communists and their leader Lenin. Orwell's book mirrors Stalin's subsequent struggle with Trotsky for leadership and his eventual control of Russia from the 1920s to the end of the Second World War.

1917	Russian Revolution
1922	Stalin becomes general secretary of the Communist Party in Russia
1924	In the UK, first Labour government forms under Ramsay MacDonald; in Russia, Lenin dies; Stalin and Trotsky struggle for power
1928	First of Stalin's Five-Year Plans
1929	Trotsky exiled from Soviet Union
1933	Hitler, leader of the Nazi Party, elected chancellor in Germany
1936–8	Stalin's Great Purge kills millions
1936–9	Spanish Civil War
1939	Stalin and Hitler sign non-aggression pact
1939–45	Second World War
1940	Trotsky assassinated on Stalin's orders
1941	Germany invades Russia
1943	Battle of Stalingrad; Tehran Conference – Roosevelt, Churchill and Stalin meet
1953	Stalin dies

Joseph Stalin

Leon Trotsky

PART TWO: PLOT AND ACTION

Plot summary: What happens in *Animal Farm*?

REVISION ACTIVITY

● Go through the summaries for the six sections below and **highlight** what you think are the **key moments**.

● Then find each moment in the **text** and **reread** it. Write down **two reasons** why you think each moment is so **important**.

CHAPTER 1

● Major, a prize-winning boar, tells the other animals on Manor Farm about a dream he has had, in which animals live free from human slavery.

● Major's speech inspires the animals to rebel against mankind and create their own society based on Major's ideas of equality and freedom.

CHAPTERS 2 AND 3

● Mr Jones, the farmer, is driven out of the farm. Mrs Jones flees too, followed by the raven Moses.

● The farm is renamed Animal Farm.

● The Seven Commandments are written on the barn wall by Snowball as a permanent reminder of the new farm rules.

● The animals discover that the pigs have taken the milk and apples for themselves.

● The animals work hard to get the harvest in and do a better job than Mr Jones ever did.

● Snowball teaches the rest of the animals to read and write.

● Napoleon takes the puppies away to be educated in private.

● Squealer tells the animals that the pigs have taken the milk and apples for everyone's benefit.

CHAPTERS 4 AND 5

● The animals try to spread the revolutionary ideas of Animal Farm across the countryside.

● Two neighbouring farmers, Mr Frederick and Mr Pilkington, are frightened that the revolution will spread to their own farms. They help Mr Jones to attack Animal Farm.

● Snowball leads the animals to victory in the Battle of the Cowshed.

● Mollie vanishes from the farm.

● The conflict between Napoleon and Snowball increases.

● After he disagrees with Napoleon about the building of the windmill, Snowball is attacked by Napoleon's dogs and driven from the farm.

● Napoleon tells the other animals that there will be no more debates – the pigs will make the decisions.

CHAPTERS 6 AND 7

- The animals work harder than ever before.
- The windmill runs into difficulties.
- Napoleon decides to trade with humans.
- The pigs move into Mr Jones's house and sleep in beds.
- The animals face starvation. Napoleon takes Mr Whymper, his solicitor, around the farm and tricks him into thinking that gossip about the famine is untrue.
- Napoleon holds a terrifying 'show trial', accusing his opponents of ludicrous 'crimes'. The accused animals are publicly executed. The other animals are frightened and confused.

CHAPTERS 8 AND 9

- The pigs continue to alter the Commandments on the wall to justify their actions.
- The animals work harder than they did under Mr Jones but eat far less.
- Napoleon's trade with Mr Frederick causes problems and the humans destroy the finished windmill.
- The new young pigs are to be educated separately.
- Moses returns to the farm.
- Boxer collapses in the quarry. The pigs sell Boxer to the knacker's yard as he is too weak to work. They use the money they get for him to buy more whisky.

CHAPTER 10

- The farm is richer than ever but the animals also work harder than ever.
- Clover sees the pigs walking on their hind legs and Napoleon carrying a whip.
- The Commandments have been erased and replaced by a single slogan: 'All Animals Are Equal But Some Animals Are More Equal Than Others'.
- The pigs invite the farmers to dinner.
- The animals look in through the farmhouse window and can no longer see the difference between the pigs and the humans.

Chapter 1: Major's dream

SUMMARY

❶ Mr Jones, the owner of Manor Farm, tries to lock the farm up for the night but is too drunk to do it properly. He then goes to bed.

❷ Major, a boar who is respected by the other farm animals, calls everyone to the barn for a meeting.

❸ Major tells the animals about a dream he has had of a future in which the animals will be able to live on the farm in freedom and peace – without being exploited by humans.

❹ Major gives the animals a set of rules for them to live by to avoid becoming like man, their enemy.

❺ Major's dream has unified the animals. Excited by what they have heard, they sing 'Beasts of England' (p. 19), which wakes Mr Jones.

❻ Mr Jones fires his gun and frightens the animals, who go back to their beds.

CHECKPOINT 1

In what ways are the animals' names appropriate? Give at least one example.

WHY IS THIS CHAPTER IMPORTANT?

A It introduces the **setting** (a farm), Mr Jones and the animals to the reader. The first animal we meet is Major, the 'Middle White' boar (p. 13).

B Orwell makes us notice the **differences** between the animals, and their behaviour in the barn gives the reader **clues** as to how the animals will behave later in the book. The animals are anthropomorphic but are still **believable** as farm animals.

C Major's speech establishes an **idealised vision** of the **future** in contrast to the animals' present **suffering** under Mr Jones – and their later suffering under the pigs.

D Orwell encourages the reader to feel **sympathetic** towards some of the animals from the start so that we appreciate just how badly the pigs behave as they gain **control** of the farm.

E Major's **revolutionary vision** predicts many events that later come true – such as Boxer's eventual fate. The irony is that this occurs under the pigs' tyranny, not man's.

CHECKPOINT 2

Are there any other ways in which Orwell makes us feel sympathetic towards the animals in Chapter 1?

KEY CONNECTION

Major's speech is based on Karl Marx's *Communist Manifesto* (1848), which he wrote with Frederick Engels. Lenin, the first Soviet leader, based many of his ideas on Marx's thinking.

MAJOR'S SPEECH

Major states that the life of the animals on the farm is one of 'misery and slavery' (p. 15) because the animals are exploited by man, their only real enemy, who 'consumes without producing' (p. 16) and doesn't reward them for what he takes.

Major's speech is based on the work of the German philosopher Karl Marx. Marx believed that capitalists behave in the same way that Major thinks the humans do, by exploiting the workers or proletariat (or in Major's case, the farm animals). The proletariat are exploited by being made to work very hard in return for minimal pay. They never see the rewards of their own labour. Marx thought that this would only stop if the proletariat revolted against the capitalists.

Orwell makes the reader feel sympathetic to this Marxist argument by listing the ways in which man makes the animals suffer. According to Major 'No animal in England is free' (p. 15). The only solution is to rebel against man. There should be 'perfect unity' as 'All animals are comrades' (p. 17).

Most importantly, the animals should never behave like man or imitate him in any way. Major suggests that the animals create a new society, based on equality, as 'All animals are equal' (p. 18).

Major's speech serves as a benchmark by which to judge the pigs' subsequent actions. The chapters that follow show how the principles of Animalism are distorted and corrupted. Major predicts many events that later come true – such as Boxer's eventual fate.

'All animals are equal'?

Although Orwell uses Major to emphasise the need for unity and equality in Chapter 1, there are signs that this is harder to achieve than the animals first think. Directly after Major's speech, the dogs attack the rats (p. 17). This seems to directly contradict what Major has just said.

The animals are not united at the start of the story: although some animals protect others, some seem intent on fighting among themselves. Some, like the cat, are simply not to be trusted at all.

Examiner's tip: Writing about the animals

As the animals enter the barn, note carefully how Orwell describes them. When writing about the characters, you should show how the descriptions in this chapter anticipate the animals' later reaction to events – don't just list what they do without explaining *why* it is significant.

For example, Boxer and Clover are shown 'walking very slowly and setting down their vast hairy hoofs with great care lest there should be some small animal concealed in the straw' (p. 14), so it comes as no surprise to the reader that they both behave compassionately later in the book and provide a contrast to the pigs' cruelty.

★ GRADE BOOSTER

Look at how Orwell subtly suggests that Major's promised utopia might never happen. Find as many examples as you can in this chapter that show that the animals' society isn't equal (for instance, the pigs make their way to the front of the meeting as though that is their natural position).

KEY QUOTE

Major: 'All animals are equal' (p. 18)

GLOSSARY

Middle White a breed of pig

Chapter 2: The rebellion

Summary

1. Following Major's death, the pigs teach his ideas to the other animals on the farm.

2. Mr Jones forgets to feed and milk the animals, who rebel against him and drive him and his men off the farm.

3. Mrs Jones flees the farm, followed by Moses.

4. Napoleon and Snowball (two young, literate boars) take charge.

5. Following Major's instructions, basic rules are established for a free and equal society.

6. The Seven Commandments are written on the wall for all to read but, despite Snowball's literacy classes, few of the animals can read them.

7. Manor Farm is renamed Animal Farm and is a more efficient and happier place than before. The animals seem to have created a perfect society.

8. While the animals are at the harvest, unbeknown to them, Napoleon attends to the milk. On their return, they find that the milk has vanished.

Why is this chapter important?

A It establishes Major's **dream**, which inspires the animals and gives them 'a completely new outlook on life' (p. 23).

B Orwell **introduces** three pigs on the farm: Napoleon, Snowball and Squealer, who are the driving force behind the planning for the Revolution. They take Major's ideas and turn them into a **philosophy** called 'Animalism' (p. 23), which is taught to the other animals.

C Support for these ideas is shown to be neither uniform nor unanimous. Some animals react with 'stupidity and apathy' (p. 24), some still feel loyal to Mr Jones. These **differences of opinion** will bring problems later on.

D Mr Jones's idle and self-indulgent behaviour and his neglect of the farm is set up so that his **expulsion from the farm** seems a good thing.

E The **Rebellion** is a 'sudden uprising' (p. 26) and happens faster than any of the animals had imagined.

A new dawn

Orwell leaves us in no doubt that the Rebellion is a good thing. The description of the farm after Mr Jones's expulsion is poetic and contains an evocative physical description of the animals' activities. This is occasionally comic – one of the first things the animals do is to gallop around the farm.

The new dawn is symbolic as well as literal. It is as though the animals have woken from a sleep. They excitedly savour the fact that it is now their farm. We are made aware of the scale of the animals' achievement: 'with speechless admiration … they could hardly believe that it was all their own' (p. 27).

The harvest shows how hard the animals have to work in their new lives but that the unity and cooperation they share makes the work much more successful.

CHECKPOINT 3

Look at the descriptions of Napoleon and Snowball. How do they prepare you for what happens later in the book?

 **GRADE BOOSTER**

The fact that the farm is called Manor Farm reminds us of the feudal system, suggesting that Jones is clinging to the past and cannot adapt to change.

CHECKPOINT 4

The animals are said to be speechless in other parts of the book too. Why is this a cause for concern?

HOUSE OF HORROR

The animals' reactions to the farmhouse are comic as well as touching. Their reluctance to enter it, and their reaction to it – they gaze at the 'unbelievable luxury' (p. 28) – emphasise their mistrust and fear of Mr Jones. The house is seen from the animals' perspective: to us, the burial of the hams is comic; to the animals, it is entirely proper. At this stage all the animals are involved in making decisions on the farm – as we see when they vote to preserve the farmhouse as a museum. Their view of the luxuries within will resonate later when Napoleon appropriates the farmhouse for his own use.

EXAMINER'S TIP: WRITING ABOUT THE SEVEN COMMANDMENTS

When the Seven Commandments are written on the barn wall, Snowball tells the animals that they form 'an unalterable law' (p. 29) for life on the farm. The Commandments are the foundations for the post-revolutionary society and their echoing of Christianity's Ten Commandments is deliberate. They provide a quasi-religious code for the animals to live by – even though most of the animals cannot read. Orwell also uses them structurally in the book to provide a framework by which we can judge the pigs' later actions and chart the farm's gradual descent into tyranny.

Chapter 3: The pigs take charge

SUMMARY

1. The harvest is completed in record time, as the animals work hard under the supervision of the pigs.

2. The animals are taught to read and write by Snowball.

3. Napoleon takes the puppies away to raise them himself.

4. Squealer tells the animals that the pigs have taken the apples and milk for everyone's benefit.

CHECKPOINT 5

What does each animal's reading ability tell you about them?

DID YOU KNOW

Orwell wrote of the moment when the pigs steal the milk and apples: 'If the other animals had the sense to put their foot down, then it would have been alright.'

★ **GRADE BOOSTER**

This chapter also satirises the uses towards which a crucial skill such as reading can be put. Find instances later in the book where Orwell suggests that this lack of ability or interest on the animals' part is a factor in their exploitation.

WHY IS THIS CHAPTER IMPORTANT?

A It shows that the **animals' behaviour** after the Rebellion is generally **unselfish** and as a result they achieve greater success than they did before.

B The tone at the start of this chapter creates a sense of **liberation** and **euphoria**, as the description of the harvest echoes the rhetoric of Major's speech.

C Boxer's **determination** is contrasted with the behaviour of Mollie and the cat, who can be described as **parasites**.

D Orwell draws the reader's attention to the fact that the revolution and issues of **equality** are not straightforward.

E We see that Snowball is an **innovator**: he organises various committees in an effort to help the animals.

F There is **conflict** between Snowball and Napoleon.

G We begin to see **Squealer**'s importance to the pigs.

UNITY AND CONFLICT

Orwell emphasises the animals' unity and creates a community in which each individual works their hardest for the group: 'Nobody stole, nobody grumbled over his rations, the quarrelling and biting and jealousy … had almost disappeared.' (p. 34). The animals' behaviour seems to have changed for the better. However, the conflict between Napoleon and Snowball begins to disrupt life on the farm. Napoleon dismisses Snowball's work and concentrates on building up his own power. We are given hints about how this is done but don't find out its full extent until later in the story.

THE CLEVERNESS OF THE PIGS

The pigs are shown to be more intelligent than other animals: 'With their superior knowledge it was natural that they should assume the leadership' (p. 33). By becoming the farm's managers, the pigs avoid physical work. At this point in the book this is not seen as sinister.

Snowball's brilliance has its flaws, though: the committees have no real function as the animals only have a limited understanding of what Snowball tells them – and this works against him in the end.

We also see how persuasive Squealer is when he defends the pigs' actions in a brilliant piece of **rhetoric** which is reinforced by his repeated threat of Mr Jones's return: 'Do you know what would happen if we pigs failed in our duty? Jones would come back!' (p. 39). Later, Squealer systematically distorts Major's commandments, reflecting the gradual erosion of the animals' revolutionary ideals. The pigs' cleverness becomes a double-edged sword: although it means Animal Farm can survive, it enables the pigs to exploit the other animals, for example, taking advantage of Boxer's gentleness to manipulate him later on.

THE IMPORTANCE OF EDUCATION

Snowball's most important task is to teach the animals to read. Although we are told that his classes are 'a great success' and 'almost every animal on the farm was literate in some degree' (p. 36) the animals fail to make the most of the skills they have been taught. Muriel reads from the rubbish dump, Benjamin says there is 'nothing worth reading' (p. 36) and Mollie simply indulges her own vanity. Boxer and Clover want to learn but don't have the ability to get beyond the basics.

Snowball's attempts to encourage the animals to participate more in the revolution prove futile.

EXAMINER'S TIP: WRITING ABOUT SNOWBALL

Snowball is seen in a less appealing light in this chapter. Look at his reaction when the windfall apples are taken and the fact that he agrees with the pigs' use of the milk. The animals, because they believe that they are living as equals, 'had assumed as a matter of course' (p. 38) that the windfall apples would be shared out, along with the milk. Orwell tells us that, despite the murmured protests of the animals, 'it was no use' (p. 38) as all the pigs are in agreement. For Orwell this was one of the central passages in the book. This is reinforced by the fact that even Mr Jones put the milk in the hens' mash rather than keep it for himself.

You could explore how far our view of Snowball is coloured by the fact that he is driven off the farm and used as a bogeyman later in the book.

CHECKPOINT 6

Why does Squealer use the word 'duty' (p. 39) when defending the pigs' actions?

 **GRADE BOOSTER**

Try researching the life of Leon Trotsky. How different to Stalin do you think he would have been as a leader?

CHECKPOINT 7

Look at the use of the word 'order' on p. 38. What is starting to happen on the farm?

Chapter 4: The Battle of the Cowshed

SUMMARY

① News of the rebellion at Animal Farm spreads. The animals try to promote the revolutionary ideas of Animal Farm across the countryside.

② The farmers of the two neighbouring farms, Mr Frederick and Mr Pilkington, frightened that their own animals will revolt, take steps to prevent an animal uprising.

③ Mr Jones attempts to recapture Animal Farm.

④ Snowball leads the animals to victory in the Battle of the Cowshed.

WHY IS THIS CHAPTER IMPORTANT?

A Orwell reminds us of what the animals are revolting against when he introduces the **humans**.

B The farmers **suppress** any signs of **rebellion** on neighbouring farms.

C Snowball is seen as a brilliant **strategist**.

D Boxer's **compassion** is emphasised when he is upset at knocking the stable-lad unconscious during the battle.

E There are further signs that a **hierarchy** is slowly developing: Napoleon and Snowball direct events on the farm and the actions of **some** animals are rewarded.

PORTRAYAL OF THE HUMANS

All the humans in the book are portrayed as being unpleasant. The farmers try to take advantage of Mr Jones's situation, while Mr Jones himself is a drunken brute. The humans' brutality reinforces Major's negative view of humanity and reminds us of what the animals have revolted against. Orwell wants us to see that the revolution was necessary.

SNOWBALL: A GREAT LEADER?

Like his allegorical counter-part, Trotsky, Snowball is seen as a capable leader. He anticipates the humans' attack and devises a carefully planned campaign in which the invaders are ambushed. Look carefully at Snowball's actions here – Napoleon later distorts these events to turn the animals against Snowball and improve his own reputation. However, we also notice Snowball's ruthless dismissal of human suffering: 'The only good human being is a dead one' (p. 45).

GRADE BOOSTER

The medals the animals receive – 'Animal Hero, First Class' and 'Animal Hero, Second Class' (p. 45) – show that already some animals are considered to be better than others. Find other instances where inequality is evident. Provide quotes to support your answers.

CHECKPOINT 8

Why are all the humans in the book so unpleasant? How does this serve Orwell's purpose in writing *Animal Farm*?

KEY QUOTE

'The only good human being is a dead one.' (p. 45)

BOXER'S REMORSE

Boxer is horrified when he thinks he might have hurt the stable-lad. He is clearly brave and prepared to defend the farm but his use of violence is not pre-meditated. He will only use as much violence as is needed to achieve his aims. This contrasts strongly with the pigs' calculated use of terror to intimidate the animals later in the book.

EXAMINER'S TIP: WRITING ABOUT THE BATTLE OF THE COWSHED

Mr Jones, with his men and some from Foxwood and Pinchfield, invade Animal Farm hoping to recapture it but the animals put up a fight. It is Snowball's finest hour. His brilliant command of the animals, his careful planning and tactics and above all his own bravery in battle are crucial to the animals' success. He is the undisputed hero of the event. The Battle of the Cowshed, as it becomes known, is to be commemorated on its anniversary by firing Mr Jones's gun.

KEY QUOTE

'But the most terrifying spectacle of all was Boxer, rearing up on his hind legs and striking out with his great iron-shod hoofs' (p. 44)

Chapter 5: Snowball flees for his life

SUMMARY

① Mollie vanishes and is rumoured to be happy in servitude under Mr Pilkington.

② The conflict between Napoleon and Snowball increases as their disagreements become more serious.

③ Snowball suggests building a windmill, which brings the farm's divisions out into the open.

④ Napoleon's dogs attack Snowball and he is forced to flee for his life.

⑤ Once he has seized power, Napoleon abolishes the Sunday debates.

⑥ Squealer tells the animals that the windmill will be built and that it was Napoleon's idea all along.

WHY IS THIS CHAPTER IMPORTANT?

A The pigs now **control** what happens on the farm; they decide 'all questions of farm policy' (p. 50).

B Plans for the windmill are simplified into **slogans** rather than discussed in reasoned speeches.

C On the allegorical level, the differing views of **socialism** held by Trotsky and Stalin are highlighted (See **Key Contexts**).

D Napoleon shows his **contempt for free speech**.

E Napoleon uses **violence** to establish absolute control over the animals.

F The Sunday Meeting, instead of being a time when the animals agree their workload, becomes the assembly at which their **orders** are given.

G The chapter ends on a much **bleaker** note than when it opened.

KEY QUOTE

'It had come to be accepted that the pigs, who were manifestly cleverer than the other animals, should decide all questions of farm policy.' (p. 50)

KEY CONNECTION

Look at how Nick Park shows animals behaving in his films, such as *The Wrong Trousers* and *Chicken Run*. Can you see any similarities with the animals' behaviour in *Animal Farm*?

★ GRADE BOOSTER

How does the use of violence and intimidation mark a watershed in the story?

NAPOLEON TIGHTENS HIS GRIP

The animals slowly begin to lose control over their lives. All decisions are taken by the pigs, although at first they claim that decisions are to be agreed by a majority vote. The animals' fickle nature (for example, changing their mind according to whoever is speaking) and their lack of intelligence make it easy for Napoleon to take control.

The sheep with their mindless bleating effectively silence opposing opinions as no one else can be heard. Napoleon symbolically assumes Major's status by standing on the platform where Major gave his speech. Napoleon has already taken his first steps towards becoming a dictator. The animals are uneasy about his actions but cannot express what they feel.

THE CAMPAIGN AGAINST SNOWBALL

Napoleon makes little response to Snowball's speeches, and when he does speak it is only to criticise Snowball. Napoleon's campaign against Snowball is carefully planned, as is demonstrated by his use of the sheep and dogs.

Snowball's exile and Napoleon's use of terror remove all opposition to the latter's plans. After Snowball's expulsion, any hope of a more just and equitable life becomes very unlikely. The farm is on its way to becoming a totalitarian society.

EXAMINER'S TIP: WRITING ABOUT SNOWBALL AND NAPOLEON

We are told that Snowball and Napoleon 'disagreed at every point where disagreement was possible' (p. 50). Snowball has many schemes which in theory would improve the life of the animals, but which would take some effort to put into practice, such as his plan for the windmill. However, his schemes seem to be for the farm's benefit rather than for his own.

Napoleon is seen to have little time for such plans – nor indeed respect for those who make them. This is most apparent in his urinating on Snowball's plans, which emphasises again his brutal and uncivilised character. Both pigs build their support among the animals in different ways.

EXAMINER'S TIP: WRITING ABOUT SQUEALER'S USE OF PROPAGANDA

Squealer's propaganda is crucial to Napoleon. He describes Napoleon as a hero, talking about his 'deep and heavy responsibility' and his 'sacrifice' (p. 55–6) and emphasising the gulf between the animals and their leader. By his skilful use of omissions and half-truths, not to mention outright lies and questionable evidence, Squealer succeeds in convincing the animals of Napoleon's fitness for power and justifying his actions. The fact that the animals rarely understand or question the meaning of his words makes his job easier. Squealer's suggestion that Napoleon has taken away the animals' rights to decision-making in case they make 'the wrong decisions' (p. 56), shows how undemocratic Animal Farm has become.

CHECKPOINT 10

What hints are there in this chapter that Napoleon has carefully planned the way in which he gains power?

? DID YOU KNOW

Adolf Hitler's Nazi government and the People's Republic of China, under Mao Zedong, are further examples of totalitarian regimes.

GRADE BOOSTER

It is a good idea to look carefully at moments when two characters have differing views. Consider who Orwell expects us to side with.

CHECKPOINT 11

In Chapter 5, how does Squealer persuade the animals to doubt their own opinions?

Chapter 6: Labour and hunger

SUMMARY

❶ The animals continue their hard labour, working a sixty-hour week and Sunday afternoons as well.

❷ The building of the windmill runs into difficulties.

❸ The harvest is poorer than the previous year.

❹ Napoleon tells the animals that he has decided to trade with the neighbouring farmers.

❺ The pigs move into the farmhouse and break the Fourth Commandment by sleeping in beds. This is explained away by Squealer as necessary for the defence of the farm. An alteration to this Commandment is painted onto the wall.

CHECKPOINT 12

How does Squealer stop the animals from questioning Napoleon's decision to trade?

❻ A storm destroys the windmill but Napoleon declares that it was sabotaged by Snowball and passes the death sentence upon him.

❼ Life for the animals continues to be hard as they try to rebuild the windmill.

WHY IS THIS CHAPTER IMPORTANT?

A The pigs use – or rather misuse – **language** to make the sufferings that they inflict upon the animals sound acceptable.

B Napoleon's announcement about **trading with other farms** is a **formality**, as plans have already been made.

C The animals' hard work brings **suffering**; Boxer starts to lose his strength.

D Orwell contrasts the **hardship** suffered by the animals with the **luxurious** lifestyle enjoyed by the pigs to point up their **corruption**.

KEY CONNECTION

Hitler used the Jews as scapegoats for Germany's economic and political problems in the 1930s. Scapegoats are usually stereotyped so that they appear as inhuman as possible to their target group.

FINDING A SCAPEGOAT

Snowball's exile provides Napoleon with a scapegoat – if any of Napoleon's plans fail, Snowball can always be blamed. A scapegoat unites the animals against a common enemy.

Napoleon tells the animals that the windmill was not destroyed by the storm but was sabotaged by Snowball and shows them the 'evidence' of Snowball's footprints. The animals believe that Napoleon is the only one who can protect them from the outside world.

DISTORTING LANGUAGE

The labour that the animals do is said to be voluntary but it is actually compulsory: if the animals don't work, they will not be fed. This distortion of language is one way in which the pigs control the farm animals (see **Language**).

REVISION ACTIVITY

The following are examples of the close ties between language and power in the book:

- **Simplification of language:** Major's statement that 'Whatever goes upon two legs, is an enemy. Whatever goes upon four legs, or has wings, is a friend.' (p. 18) is reduced to the slogan 'Four legs good, two legs bad' (p. 37). This loss of meaning becomes dangerous when the sheep chant the slogan to drown opposition to Napoleon (p. 55, for instance).

- **Inarticulate opposition:** Clover's inability to articulate her own feelings (p. 80) means that she has to resort to singing 'Beasts of England' to mark her sadness – an ineffective form of protest.

Can you think of any others?

EXAMINER'S TIP: WRITING ABOUT LANGUAGE

This chapter shows the gradual but definite grasp of power by the pigs as 'the animals worked like slaves' (p. 61). Orwell's use of irony directs our attention to what is really happening. The animals' pride that their work is 'for the benefit of themselves' and not for 'idle, thieving human beings' (p. 61) is undercut by our awareness that the animals are being exploited in exactly this way by the pigs.

KEY CONNECTION

The idea of how governments can use language to control people is developed in Orwell's last book *Nineteen Eighty-Four*.

KEY QUOTE

Squealer: 'A bed merely means a place to sleep in … The rule was against sheets, which are a human invention.' (p. 66)

KEY QUOTE

'Again the animals seemed to remember that a resolution against this had been passed in the early days, and again Squealer was able to convince them that this was not the case.' (p. 65)

Chapter 7: Napoleon's reign of terror

SUMMARY

1. The animals face starvation.

2. The windmill is rebuilt (with thicker walls) but work is slow.

3. Napoleon takes Mr Whymper, his solicitor, around the farm and tricks him into thinking that the rumours of famine are untrue.

4. The hens, angry that their eggs are being sold to Whymper, rebel.

5. Napoleon decides to sell some timber and conducts separate negotiations with Mr Pilkington and Mr Frederick.

6. Four pigs and three hens, among others, are executed in front of the other terrified animals.

WHY IS THIS CHAPTER IMPORTANT?

A. The terrible weather mentioned at the start of the chapter reinforces the **harsh realities** of life for the animals.

B. **Duplicitous** Napoleon **tricks** the other farmers into believing that the animals are **happy** and contented and that food is **plentiful**.

C. The hens' refusal to hand over their eggs for sale forms the first serious internal **challenge** to Napoleon's power.

D. Napoleon decides to sell some timber and conducts **negotiations** with Mr Pilkington and Mr Frederick but never both at the same time.

E. The pigs feel confident enough to **rewrite history**, telling the animals that Snowball was a coward at the Battle of the Cowshed.

F. The executions that Napoleon organises parallel Stalin's violent elimination of his opponents during the 1920s and 1930s (see **Key Contexts**). Napoleon's cruelty is emphasised by his disproportionately brutal and unexpected **violence**.

KEY QUOTE

'Starvation seemed to stare them in the face.' (p. 71)

CHECKPOINT 13

How does Orwell describe the executions and what effect does this have?

GRADE BOOSTER

Orwell shifts from his use of the third person narrative to Clover's unspoken thoughts and feelings. What effect does this have on the reader? Think about why Orwell does this.

KEY QUOTE

'Whenever anything went wrong it became usual to attribute it to Snowball.' (p. 74)

STUNNED INTO SILENCE?

After the executions, Clover can't think or voice her objections to what has just happened. She still trusts the pigs – showing how successfully the pigs have brainwashed the animals.

All Clover can do, as she 'lacked the words' (p. 80) to protest, is sing 'Beasts of England'. The song becomes a substitute for language and is then banned because its references to a better world could be seen as subversive. It is replaced with a worthless anthem.

TERROR AND CONTROL

The success of Napoleon and Squealer's techniques is clear to us: the condemned animals confess to non-existent crimes. Almost as horrifying as the executions is the fact that although the farm animals are terrified by the slaughter, they believe that the victims were traitors.

We see other techniques in this chapter: supposed sabotage is used again as a pretext by Napoleon to remove his opposition. His tactics also point up the gullibility of the animals and their readinesss to accept what they are told; for example, when Napoleon appears to be about to sell the timber to Pilkington, the animals are told that Snowball is living on Frederick's farm and vice versa.

EXAMINER'S TIP: WRITING ABOUT NAPOLEON

Napoleon is now rarely seen and is referred to as 'Our Leader, Comrade Napoleon' (p. 76). Squealer creates an image of Napoleon as a wise, heroic leader. Napoleon is said to be a brave and successful fighter. He awards himself medals and his appearances become mainly ceremonial. Squealer becomes more and more important as the only means of communication between Napoleon and the other animals. Even the most stupid of the animals question the executions but Squealer is again able to answer them. The animals' trust in the pigs is another reason for Napoleon's success.

EXAMINER'S TIP: WRITING ABOUT ORWELL'S TECHNIQUES

The detailed description of the farm and the emphasis on its beauty is used by Orwell to create an image of what the animals have lost and how the revolution could have turned out. He juxtaposes two different visions in this chapter: the ideal of the possible freedom and peace that the animals could have achieved is set against the terrifying reality of their lives. The reader is reminded of what the revolution originally set out to do and how these revolutionary ideals have been betrayed by the pigs' corruption of Major's ideas.

CHECKPOINT 14

Why don't the animals protest at this point?

KEY QUOTE

'they had come to a time when no one dared speak his mind, when fierce growling dogs roamed everywhere, and when you had to watch your comrades torn to pieces after confessing to shocking crimes.' (p. 80)

CHECKPOINT 15

Does Napoleon deserve his medals? Why does he award them to himself and what does this show?

**GRADE BOOSTER**

Make careful notes on the differences between Squealer's account of the Battle of the Cowshed and that given earlier in the book.

Chapter 8: The Battle of the Windmill

SUMMARY

① It is clear that the Seven Commandments are being altered.

② The animals are working even harder and eating less than under Mr Jones.

③ The windmill is finished.

④ Napoleon finally sells the timber to Frederick, who pays with forged notes. When he realises that Frederick has tricked him, Napoleon passes the death sentence on the farmer.

⑤ Frederick then invades the farm and destroys the windmill. The Battle of the Windmill is won by the animals but only just.

⑥ The pigs find a crate of whisky.

WHY IS THIS CHAPTER IMPORTANT?

A Napoleon's **abuse of power** becomes more **blatant**. Any animals who defy him are slaughtered, the rest are terrified by his dogs.

B Orwell reminds us that the animals' lives are **worsening** under Napoleon. Following the aftermath of the executions, the dogs are a threatening presence on the farm and the animals face daily **hardships**.

C Napoleon now lives in even greater **comfort**, and seems to ignore Major's assertion that 'all the habits of Man are evil' (p. 18).

D The animals are left **demoralised** at the end of this chapter as the building of the windmill proves to be **futile**.

E Squealer's **statistics** bear no relation to the food that the animals are given, highlighting the gap between his **lies and reality**.

IRONY AND THE NARRATOR

From the animals' viewpoint, the discovery of Squealer, collapsed with a pot of paint and a brush at the foot of the wall, is a 'strange incident which hardly anyone was able to understand' (p. 94). To us, it is clear that Squealer alters the Commandments as the pigs break them – he is literally rewriting history. This episode is a good example of Orwell's use of the narrator to create irony.

BLIND TRUST

Squealer is caught red-handed altering the Commandments, yet the animals still don't see what is happening to them; they don't even trust the evidence of their own eyes. The animals are so used to having others think for them that they can't think for themselves. The pigs' confidence in their own power means that they make even less effort to cover their tracks.

KEY CONNECTION

Watch the animated version of *Animal Farm*. Does the film place the emphasis on events that you would expect?

★ **GRADE BOOSTER**

Where else in the book do you see Orwell using the narrator to create irony?

KEY QUOTE

'Even Napoleon, who was directing operations from the rear, had the tip of his tail chipped by a pellet.' (p. 91)

REVISION ACTIVITY

In Orwell's last novel *Nineteen Eighty-Four*, IngSoc, the totalitarian regime, uses 'doublethink' to control the behaviour of its people, by removing their freedom to think for themselves. Can you see any similarities between the techniques used by IngSoc in *Nineteen Eighty-Four* and the pigs in *Animal Farm*? What does this tell you about Orwell's concerns and his motivation for writing these books?

EXAMINER'S TIP: WRITING ABOUT THE BATTLE OF THE WINDMILL

The Battle of the Windmill is one of the few times when we see the animals fighting for a common cause. Their actions contrast sharply with those at the Battle of the Cowshed. The pain and effort involved in this later battle are stressed by Orwell. Squealer's complete misrepresentation of the Battle of the Windmill shows that the pigs' distortion of events is becoming complete. Not only are events in the distant past altered, but recent history too. The celebrations following the battle are used to divert the animals' attention from the forged banknotes.

REVISION ACTIVITY

How do dictators keep power? Think about:

- **The removal of democracy:** The abolition of debates and elections removes a valuable way for the animals to express their opinions.

- **Terror:** The bloodbath in the barn and the executions that follow remind us of the most primitive way of maintaining power – terror.

- **The control of information:** All information is carefully managed by the pigs to hide their real aims. The lack of any other source of information means that the animals have no way of checking the truth.

- **Propaganda:** Napoleon uses Squealer's abilities to 'turn black into white' (p. 23) to brainwash the farm animals into accepting his decisions and actions.

Can you think of any other methods used in the story?

Chapter 9: Boxer's death

SUMMARY

❶ Boxer's hoof takes a long time to heal but he refuses to do less work.

❷ Life on the farm is very hard: the animals are starving as rations have been reduced even further.

❸ The young pigs are to be educated in a separate schoolroom.

❹ Moses returns to the farm.

❺ Boxer collapses in the quarry and is sold by the pigs to the knacker's yard.

❻ The pigs use the money they have been paid for Boxer's corpse to buy another crate of whisky and have a memorial banquet for the horse.

WHY IS THIS CHAPTER IMPORTANT?

A The rumours about the use of an area of pasture for retired animals show how much the animals now rely on **rumour** rather than fact.

B The farm's **inequality** is clear in the comparison between the hungry and cold animals, whose lives are 'harsh and bare' (p. 98) and the pigs, who 'were putting on weight if anything' (p. 99).

C Moses returns to the farm with tales of 'Sugarcandy Mountain' (p. 101), showing that the animals again have to resort to the **hope** of an afterlife rather than face the **realities** of their lives.

D We also realise how much Boxer has **sacrificed** for the revolution.

E Major's **prophecy** of Boxer's end is **fulfilled** – though in a far worse way than he predicted.

PARADES AND PROPAGANDA

The pigs divert attention from the animals' hardship and the elitism on the farm through the use of parades, songs and propaganda. Squealer uses words in ways that completely contradict their meaning, such as the 'Spontaneous Demonstration' (p. 100), which is carefully organised, and the 'Republic' (p. 100) which has only one candidate for election: Napoleon. When the animals' rations have to be reduced, Squealer refers to the change 'as a "readjustment", never as a "reduction"'.

A BLEAK FUTURE?

The piglets are trained to continue the pigs' dominance over the other animals. The prospects for the future look bleak as, even if Napoleon were to die, other pigs are ready to assume leadership. The return of Moses suggests that the other animals are – at best – back where they started.

GRADE BOOSTER

At the start, Moses is seen to be Mr Jones's pet – in the same way that the Russian Orthodox Church supported the Tsar. Why do the pigs allow Moses to return?

CHECKPOINT 16

Look at the reference to the pigs' tails on p. 99. Compare this with what Snowball told Mollie about ribbons in Chapter 2.

GRADE BOOSTER

The raven Moses represents the role of the Church and organised religion. The visions of Sugarcandy Mountain, naive and comic to us, represent Marx's view of religion as the 'opiate of the masses' – the promise of a perfect life in the future, distracting people from trying to change their present suffering.

CHECKPOINT 17

A republic is a country that elects its leaders. Do you think that Animal Farm is a republic?

FAILED BY HIS FRIENDS?

Boxer's death is the emotional climax of the book (more so than the executions) and provides another significant stepping stone in the story. It is one of the first times we see Benjamin's devotion to his friend but we also realise what the revolution has cost Boxer, who has sacrificed his health – and life – for the success of Animal Farm.

The animals' inability to help Boxer until it is too late suggests that events would never have taken this turn had they been more involved at the start of the revolution instead of relying on the pigs to take control. Orwell shows us that the farm animals' blind faith in the pigs and their inability to oppose them has terrible consequences.

EXAMINER'S TIP: WRITING ABOUT BOXER'S DEATH

Boxer's slaughter at the hands of the knacker is the most powerful event in *Animal Farm*, showing us how the pigs have betrayed the animals' trust. Their total indifference to Boxer's suffering emphasises their ruthlessness. The animals' blind faith in the pigs and their inability to oppose them has fatal consequences. While the animals are starving, the pigs have a banquet paid for by the death of their most devoted follower, which demonstrates their absolute corruption and cruelty. Take careful note of the language Orwell uses at this point. You could explore how it differs from the language Orwell uses during the executions.

KEY QUOTE

'... from somewhere or other the pigs had acquired the money to buy themselves another case of whisky.' (p. 107)

Chapter 10: The dream betrayed

SUMMARY

① Many years have passed. Few of the old animals still survive; the younger ones don't understand Animalism.

② The windmill has been restored and another one is being built.

③ Although the farm is richer, the animals work harder than ever. Napoleon now has complete control over the other animals.

④ Clover is horrified to see the pigs walking on their hind legs. Other pigs emerge from the farmhouse – including Napoleon, who is carrying a whip.

⑤ The Commandments have been erased from the barn wall and replaced by a single slogan (see **Key Quote**).

⑥ The pigs wear clothes, smoke and read newspapers.

⑦ The pigs invite the farmers to dinner.

⑧ The animals are appalled that they can no longer distinguish between the faces of the humans and the pigs. The pigs' transformation is complete.

KEY QUOTE

'ALL ANIMALS ARE EQUAL BUT SOME ANIMALS ARE MORE EQUAL THAN OTHERS.'
(p. 114)

WHY IS THIS CHAPTER IMPORTANT?

A The only animals who seem to **profit** from the farm are the pigs.

B Despite the fact that none of the benefits they had expected have arrived, the animals still **hope** that some day they will be free.

C The removal of the Seven Commandments and the **imposition** of a single nonsensical **slogan** show how thoroughly the revolution has been **corrupted**.

D Major's **hopes** of a free and equal society are seen to be just as he described them – a 'dream' (p. 15).

E The fact that Napoleon carries a whip – seen at the opening of the book as a symbol of man's vicious **oppression** – suggests that a **violent future** lies ahead.

F We see that the revolution has brought the animals **back to where they started** – they have only changed masters.

CHECKPOINT 18

Napoleon states that 'The truest happiness … lay in working hard and living frugally' (p. 110). In what ways do the pigs fail to live up to this?

BACK TO THE START?

Much of the impact of this chapter (and indeed the book) is created through parallels with the start of the story. The sheep now bleat 'Four legs good. Two legs better' (p. 113), showing how an unthinking mob can prop up a **tyrant**.

After Boxer's death, the pigs' adoption of human behaviour is rapid. Clover's horrified neighing when she sees Squealer walking on his hind legs highlights the shock at what has gradually happened to the animals. The arrival of humans on the farm emphasises the complete overthrow of every one of Major's instructions.

By the end of the book, the pigs are indistinguishable from the humans – Napoleon even looks like Mr Jones and tells the farmers that the farm will revert to its pre-revolutionary name: Manor Farm.

WORSE THAN MAN

Far from having nothing to do with man, as Major ordered, the pigs have actually surpassed man, as is clear when Mr Pilkington congratulates Napoleon on managing to run a farm in a crueller way than he does – and Napoleon says that further restrictions are planned. If anything, the pigs are worse: they have systematically violated the Commandments while claiming to support the revolution and have abused the animals' trust, leaving them in a worse position than at the start of the book.

> **? DID YOU KNOW**
>
> Orwell wrote *Animal Farm* at the height of Britain's alliance with Russia (which is reflected here in the relationship between Mr Pilkington and Napoleon). This is one reason why it was so difficult for him to get *Animal Farm* published.

> **KEY QUOTE**
>
> 'If you have your lower animals to contend with … we have our lower classes.' (p. 116)

EXAMINER'S TIP: WRITING ABOUT CLOVER

We see the final scene in the book through Clover's eyes. Orwell often uses Clover's viewpoint and a shift in tone to give us an insight into a significant moment in the text. When Clover witnesses the pigs walking on their hind legs, Orwell uses one sentence paragraphs to drive home the shock of such a sight (p. 112–13).

In this chapter, Clover's perspective is reinforced by a change in tone to a dream sequence in the final paragraph, which is reminiscent of Major's dream but remains inconclusive.

As readers, we trust Clover's view of events – Orwell ensures that we are sympathetic to Clover from the start of the story, when her maternal instinct is highlighted – and we are therefore shocked to witness the pigs' final betrayal of Animalism.

Progress and revision check

REVISION ACTIVITY

❶ What does Major say will happen to the hens' eggs? (Write your answers below)

....

❷ Why does Napoleon place himself in front of the milk buckets?

....

❸ What rumours do Mr Frederick and Mr Pilkington try to spread about life on Animal Farm?

....

❹ What song is banned by the pigs? Why?

....

❺ Who is blamed for the destruction of the first windmill?

....

REVISION ACTIVITY

Write down answers to these questions:

● What are the early indications that suggest that Napoleon will seize power?

  Start: *We know Napoleon will seize power as …*

● Individually, what does each animal's name represent? Why did Orwell choose the names that he did for the animals?

  Start: *The animals' names represent …*

GRADE BOOSTER

Answer this longer, practice question about the plot/action of the story:

Q: How complex is the structure of *Animal Farm*?

Think about:
● The way in which the Seven Commandments are violated

● The renaming of Manor Farm

● Napoleon's life by the end of the book

● What we usually expect from a fairy story or fable

For a C grade: Convey your ideas clearly and appropriately (you could use the words from the question to guide your answer) and refer to details from the text (use specific examples).

For an A grade: Make sure you comment on the varied ways the story is structured and, if possible, come up with your own or alternative ideas.

PART THREE: CHARACTERS

Snowball

WHO IS SNOWBALL?

Snowball is the farm's intellectual and he rivals Napoleon for leadership of Animal Farm.

WHAT DOES SNOWBALL DO IN THE BOOK?

- Snowball energetically promotes the revolution and teaches the animals new skills.
- Although Snowball appears to care for the well-being of the other animals, he also supports Napoleon's seizure of the apples.
- Snowball is brave in battle and a brilliant strategist. He is the mastermind behind the windmill.
- For all his brilliance, Snowball does not notice Napoleon's steady climb to power – or the use he makes of the dogs.
- Snowball is nearly killed by Napoleon's dogs and flees from the farm.

HOW IS SNOWBALL DESCRIBED AND WHAT DOES IT MEAN?

Quotation	Means?
'Snowball was ... quicker in speech and more inventive' (p. 23)	Snowball is seen as charismatic and a brilliant thinker and communicator.
'He formed the Egg Production Committee ..., the Clean Tails League ..., the Wild Comrades' Re-education Committee' (p. 36)	Snowball is dedicated to spreading Major's revolutionary ideas and teaching the animals to run the farm themselves but the comic nature of his committees suggests that his approach is theoretical and impractical – and likely to fail.
'Four legs good, two legs bad' (p. 37)	Snowball is the first to simplify language on Animal Farm.
'The only good human being is a dead one' (p. 45)	Snowball's ruthlessness makes us wonder how different the revolution would have been under him.

EXAMINER'S TIP: WRITING ABOUT SNOWBALL

You might be asked to contrast Snowball's character with Napoleon's. In Chapter 2, they are linked: Snowball's plans and ideals seem to put Napoleon in the shade. In contrast to the more talkative Snowball, Napoleon is relatively silent but equally ambitious. Napoleon and Snowball have differing ideas about Animalism – their disagreements parallel those of Stalin and Trotsky (see **Key Contexts**).

★ **GRADE BOOSTER**

Snowball is presented by Orwell as a Trotsky-like idealist who is outmanoeuvred by his calculating and utterly ruthless rival, Napoleon. Make a list of what Snowball does up until his expulsion from the farm and contrast this with Napoleon's actions. Why do you think Snowball ultimately fails to gain power?

? DID YOU KNOW

After he gained power, Stalin had Trotsky (and many other opponents) airbrushed from photographs after their murders in an attempt to erase them from history.

★ **GRADE BOOSTER**

'Whenever anything went wrong, it became usual to attribute it to Snowball.' (p. 74) How far is our reaction to Snowball shaped by his demonisation?

Napoleon

WHO IS NAPOLEON?

Napoleon is the pig who seizes control of Animal Farm after Mr Jones is expelled. Based on Joseph Stalin, he systematically destroys all of Major's ideals as he gradually adopts the behaviour and vices of the humans that Major attacked so viciously. He is a typical dictator.

WHAT DOES NAPOLEON DO IN THE BOOK?

- Napoleon takes control of the food supply quickly to get the animals' support.

- Napoleon removes the puppies and expels Snowball, demonstrating for the first time the extent of his power.

- Napoleon does not participate in the Battle of the Cowshed but later rewrites history to portray himself as a heroic leader.

- Napoleon uses Squealer to pacify the animals and disguise his rise to power.

- The extent of Napoleon's cruelty is apparent in his treatment of Boxer.

- Napoleon becomes more selfish as the story progresses – or less concerned with hiding his selfishness. By the end of the story, he has taken Jones's place almost entirely – but is worse because he has betrayed the revolution and the animals on the farm.

- Napoleon blames Snowball for his own mistakes and creates an atmosphere of hysteria in which animals will confess to the most ludicrous crimes.

EXAMINER'S TIP: WRITING ABOUT NAPOLEON

Napoleon's increasing preoccupation with his position and status demonstrates that he uses the revolution for his own gain. The Seven Commandments are rewritten throughout the story to suit Napoleon's aims. He announces his intentions to the animals, who are terrified into silent agreement, when it is clear that his plans have already been made. He keeps himself away from the other animals, lives in luxury (dining from Crown Derby china, eating sugar and drinking alcohol) and stages elaborate ceremonies in his own honour. He even has his portrait painted by Squealer. It's possible to argue that Napoleon never subscribed to the ideas expressed in Major's dream.

How is Napoleon described and what does it mean?

Quotation	Means?
He is a 'fierce-looking' boar with 'a reputation for getting his own way'. (p. 23)	He is ambitious. This quote also foreshadows the brutal way he will seize power.
Napoleon 'seemed to be biding his time'. (p. 51)	His rise to power is premeditated.
'Napoleon acted swiftly and ruthlessly.' (p. 73)	Napoleon has become a dictator, breaking Major's instructions that 'no animal must ever tyrannize over his own kind' and 'No animal must ever kill any other animal.'
'Napoleon rarely appeared in public, but spent all his time in the farmhouse, which was guarded at each door by fierce-looking dogs.' (p. 72)	Contrary to Major's spirit of equality, Napoleon has separated himself from the other animals, sleeps in the farmhouse (breaking another of Major's rules) and resorts to intimidation.
'Napoleon had denounced such ideas as contrary to the spirit of Animalism. The truest happiness, he said, lay in working hard and living frugally.' (p. 110)	Napoleon inverts the true meaning of Animalism. He is a hypocrite, claiming animals should live frugally while he lives in luxury.

GRADE BOOSTER

Find two more quotations about Napoleon. Draw your own table and write in the second column what you think each of your quotations means.

Revision Activity

Look carefully at the parallels that are made between life under Mr Jones (in Chapters 1 and 2) and life under Napoleon (Chapters 9 and 10):

- The animals are fed very little (p. 98)
- The pigs drink alcohol, as Jones did (p. 99)
- Moses the Raven reappears on the farm (p. 101)
- The pigs walk on two legs (p. 112)
- The pigs read newspapers (p. 114)

Can you find any more examples?

GRADE BOOSTER

Make a list of the ways in which Napoleon uses or manipulates each of the other animals on the farm. Find quotes to support each point.

Squealer

WHO IS SQUEALER?

Squealer is Napoleon's propagandist, his 'spin doctor', who justifies Napoleon's seizure of power.

WHAT DOES SQUEALER DO IN THE BOOK?

- Squealer is responsible for the devious changes to the Commandments.

- Squealer confuses the animals and makes them doubt their own memories, persuading them that he is right.

- Squealer gives the animals meaningless lists of statistics to convince them that life under Napoleon is getting better.

- Squealer uses his own eloquence and Napoleon's brutal dogs to enforce Napoleon's message.

- Squealer grows fatter as the story progresses, as he benefits from working for Napoleon.

? DID YOU KNOW

Squealer's name is significant as it is both an unpleasant, shrill noise made by a pig and a slang term for betrayal. He is said to represent Vyacheslav Molotov, Stalin's Prime Minister and supporter.

HOW IS SQUEALER DESCRIBED AND WHAT DOES IT MEAN?

Quotation	Means?
We are told that he is a 'brilliant talker' who can 'turn black into white' (p. 23)	He dishonestly defends the pigs' actions in brilliant pieces of rhetoric, which are often underlined by the threat of Jones's return. The animals therefore have little option but to agree to the pigs' actions.
He is 'unaccountably … absent' (p. 92) from the fighting.	This quote implies that Squealer is a coward.
'No one believes more firmly than Comrade Napoleon that all animals are equal … But sometimes you might make the wrong decisions, comrades, and then where would we be?' (p. 56)	He convinces the animals that Napoleon is acting in their best interests despite the fact that Napoleon is doing the very opposite.

Quotation	Means?
'Squealer, temporarily stunned, was sprawling beside it, and near at hand there lay a lantern, a paint-brush and an overturned pot of white paint.' (p. 94–5)	Squealer has been caught altering the Commandments on the wall to fit the pigs' actions – as he has done throughout the story. He has fallen off his ladder and Orwell suggests he is drunk – thus breaking the very Commandment he is altering.
'he cast a very ugly look at Boxer' (p. 77)	This – and the attack on the gentle Boxer that follows – highlights the sinister side to Squealer's character. His role is to ensure that any opposition to Napoleon is eliminated.

EXAMINER'S TIP

Don't just tell the examiner what Orwell does. Explain why he does it and what effect it has on the reader.

EXAMINER'S TIP: WRITING ABOUT SQUEALER

Orwell uses Squealer to demonstrate how politicians use language to control people, a theme he develops in *Nineteen Eighty-Four*. Squealer's 'shrill voice', 'twinkling eyes' and other mannerisms (p. 23) emphasise the persuasiveness of this character. He is like the modern spin doctor, presenting events and ideas in the form that best suits Napoleon's ideas.

The sinister side to Squealer's character is apparent when he is seen noting the signs of resistance to Napoleon – even when these arrive in the form of gentle questions from characters such as Boxer. His ugly sideways looks and the subsequent attack on Boxer suggest that Squealer's propaganda is more sinister than simply ensuring that the animals obey Napoleon: it is also used to eliminate anyone who doubts him. Squealer's arrogance and contempt for the other animals show the dismissive attitude that the propagandist has towards those he exploits.

REVISION ACTIVITY

Write a list, with examples, of the techniques that Squealer uses to justify Napoleon's actions to the animals.

Boxer

WHO IS BOXER?

Boxer the carthorse is 'an enormous beast' (p. 14), the revolution's most loyal disciple who is prepared to make huge sacrifices for the farm's success. He represents the proletariat and their hopes for a better world.

WHAT DOES BOXER DO IN THE BOOK?

- Boxer is a loyal supporter of the revolution. He passes on the pigs' teachings to the other animals and is 'unfailing' in his attendance at the farm meetings.

- Boxer gives up the hat he uses to protect him from flies, unlike Mollie who holds on to her ribbons.

- Boxer's strength and total commitment are vital to the success of the harvest – and the revolution.

- Boxer's integrity and honesty are shown by his defence of Snowball, which marks him out to Squealer. His strength saves him from the dogs when they attack him at the show trial.

- Boxer insists on working until he sees the windmill rebuilt.

- Boxer believes the pigs' promises of a happy retirement but is sold to the knacker.

HOW IS BOXER DESCRIBED AND WHAT DOES IT MEAN?

Quotation	Means?
'You, Boxer, the very day that those great muscles of yours lose their power, Jones will send you to the knacker, who will cut your throat and boil you down for the fox-hounds.' (p. 17)	Major's words prove prophetic for Boxer – though the irony is that this happens under Napoleon rather than Mr Jones. Even when he is being driven to the knacker's yard, Boxer has to be told what is happening to him.
'I have no wish to take life, not even human life,' repeated Boxer, and his eyes were full of tears.' (p. 45)	For all his 'terrifying' fighting during the Battle of the Cowshed, Boxer's compassion and humility are also apparent. He is devastated when he thinks he has killed the stable-lad and makes it clear that he does not want to kill even his most fervent enemy. His brave, gentle nature is used by Orwell as a contrast to Napoleon's cowardly thuggery.

Quotation	Means?
'His two slogans, "I will work harder" and "Napoleon is always right", seemed to him a sufficient answer to all problems.' (p. 62)	Boxer's unquestioning faith in the pigs enables them to – literally – get away with murder.
It must be due to some fault in ourselves.' (p. 79)	Boxer's blind faith in the pigs is seen as disastrous. Even after the dogs attack him and he sees the massacre of the animals on the farm, Boxer (who is upset by what he has seen) does not blame the pigs, and resolves to work harder. His inability to recognise the pigs' corruption is given by Orwell as another reason for Napoleon's success in his quest for power.

EXAMINER'S TIP: WRITING ABOUT BOXER

Boxer is one of the characters that we feel most sympathy for in the book. He is a loyal and dedicated follower of an ideal that he does not fully understand. His lack of intelligence and unquestioning trust in the pigs mean that he is vulnerable to their exploitation. This does not just result in suffering: according to Orwell, such behaviour is fatal. The final insult is the pigs' banquet at which they toast Boxer with whisky – forbidden by Major – which has been bought with the proceeds of his death. Even in death, Boxer is used to the pigs' advantage.

REVISION ACTIVITY

Boxer's innocent faith in the pigs and his lack of intelligence allow Napoleon to exploit him. What might have happened if Boxer had been able to see through Napoleon's plans?

Clover

WHO IS CLOVER?

Like Boxer, Clover represents the proletariat. Clover is a loyal disciple of the Animalist revolution, right to the end of the story. She criticises Mollie for her betrayal of Major's ideals.

WHAT DOES CLOVER DO IN THE BOOK?

- Clover is the only character whose thoughts we are given in detail.

- Clover is not as strong as Boxer, but she is slightly more intelligent (p. 36).

- Clover checks the Commandments as the pigs take control of the farm but never acts upon her doubts.

- Clover trusts the pigs and doubts her own memory. Her obedient nature is easily exploited by Squealer.

- Clover sees the pigs walking on their hind legs and the farmers playing cards with Napoleon.

GRADE BOOSTER

Clover is the tender heart of the book and, together with Boxer, provides an emotional core to the story that prevents it from being a dry allegory. What techniques does Orwell use to make Clover a sympathetic character?

GRADE BOOSTER

Clover is a significant character for the reader and we see the final transformation of the pigs (Chapter 10) through her eyes. How does this add to the effectiveness of the final scene? Would the scene work as well if a different character witnessed it?

Quotation	Means?
'Clover made a sort of wall around them with her great foreleg, and the ducklings nestled down inside it, and promptly fell asleep.' (p. 14)	Clover is kind and protective – a maternal presence. At the opening of the book she shelters the ducklings 'which had lost their mother' (p. 14); and in the same way, after the executions, 'The animals huddled about Clover' (p. 79).
'Clover treated the hoof with poultices of herbs which she prepared by chewing them, and both she and Benjamin urged Boxer to work less hard.' (p. 97)	She cares tenderly for Boxer when he splits his hoof and pleads with him not to overwork. She also cares for him when he collapses (p. 102–3). Clover demonstrates the tenderness that is destroyed by the pigs.
'There was no thought of rebellion or disobedience in her mind.' (p. 80)	Clover's limited intelligence and her reluctance to confront her doubts prevent her from rebelling or challenging the pigs' rule. Even after the executions she still feels loyal to the pigs.

EXAMINER'S TIP: WRITING ABOUT CLOVER

By the end of the story, Clover is exhausted and overworked – at the age of fourteen, with her rheumy eyes, she still works as hard as at the start of the book. Her deterioration mirrors that of the farm. Her journey in the story shows how ordinary people lose their freedom in small steps. At the book's conclusion it is through Clover's eyes that we see the final blurring of pig and human.

Major

Major is a 'highly regarded' pig who is a natural leader. He is twelve years old and has 'a wise and benevolent appearance' (p. 13).

- Major's speech prophesises much of what will happen on the farm in many ways – the **irony** being that it happens under Napoleon, not Jones.

- Major makes a revolutionary speech that is a mix of Marxism and Leninism, establishing the theoretical basis of the book – the struggle against tyranny for a free and equal society.

- The pigs develop Major's ideas and then pervert them, as Stalin took Lenin's doctrines and twisted them for his own benefit.

- In Chapter 10, Napoleon states that the animals would no longer march past Major's skull, highlighting the gulf between Major's aims and those of Napoleon.

- Ultimately, Major's speech sets the benchmark by which Napoleon's actions are judged by the reader.

GRADE BOOSTER

Major's political ideas are explained subtly as he suggests a utopian vision of a society in which cruelty and suffering are distant memories. In this way complex political ideas are presented in a readable form. Examine the instructions he gives the animals and compare this with the book's final chapter.

Benjamin

Benjamin the donkey is introduced as 'the oldest animal on the farm, and the worst tempered' (p. 14). Orwell uses Benjamin to show what happens to those who see wrongdoing but do nothing to stop it.

- Unlike the other animals, Benjamin questions whether the animals really will be better off as a result of the revolution.

- At the Battle of the Cowshed Benjamin is in the thick of the fighting.

- Benjamin repeatedly refuses to read the Commandments, believing that it will create trouble.

- Benjamin refuses to interfere when he sees the pigs' wrongdoing.

- When Boxer is driven to his death, Benjamin alerts the others – but by that stage it is too late to help.

- Benjamin and Clover are outside the farmhouse when the true extent of the pigs' betrayal is revealed.

GRADE BOOSTER

Can you find two ways in which Benjamin's actions contradict his views about life on the farm? What does this tell us about him?

Mr Jones

Mr Jones is the farmer who owns Manor Farm but is incapable of running it. He represents the Tsar, as well as demonstrating how capitalists exploit the working classes. His cruelty is stressed in Major's speech, and the thoughtless nature of his violence is apparent in his random shooting to quell the noise from the barn.

- After the revolution, Jones complains about it in the pub.
- Jones tries to recapture the farm but is humiliated when he lands in the manure heap.
- Jones ends up dying 'in an inebriates' home', a pathetic character.

Mollie

Mollie 'the foolish, pretty white mare' (p. 14), represents the White Russians, who had a privileged life under the Tsar. She is not committed to the revolution as she doesn't want to lose her privileges.

- She oversleeps, complains of 'mysterious pains' and is workshy.
- Mollie seems fascinated and envious of the luxuries acquired by the humans and hankers after them.

Moses

As the religious connotations of his name suggest, Moses the raven represents the Russian Orthodox Church.

- Moses convinces many of the animals that there is a better life on Sugarcandy Mountain.
- These animals therefore accept their sufferings as a temporary trial to be endured before they find eternal peace and happiness.

Minor characters

THE DOGS

- The dogs are the counterpart of Stalin's secret police.
- From the start, they are loyal animals. They are closely linked to the pigs, and later wag their tails at Napoleon in the same way that they did at Mr Jones.
- During Major's speech the dogs chase the rats and are prevented by Major from harming them as he says it is contrary to the rules of Animalism.
- Along with the pigs, the dogs are rewarded for dealing ruthlessly with any objectors and murdering Napoleon's opposition.

THE SHEEP

- The sheep represent the most stupid elements of society, the 'mob'. They are generally referred to as an anonymous group – there is no named individual who stands out.

- Their understanding of the aims of the revolution is limited to mindlessly bleating out the slogan 'Four legs good, two legs bad' (p. 37), and when Squealer decides to alter this, it takes them a week to learn the new version.

- The damage that such **indoctrination** can do is apparent at the Sunday meetings, when they drown out Snowball's speech and when they stifle the only likely moment of protest when Napoleon is seen walking along with a whip in his trotter (p. 113).

THE HENS

- The hens are the only group that attempts to show any resistance to Napoleon.

- In his speech, Major specifically criticises the taking of the hens' eggs and demands that this inhumane practice be stopped, yet under Napoleon, the hens are told to surrender their eggs.

- They retaliate by smashing their eggs, in the same way that the **kulaks** destroyed their own farms rather than let Stalin's government take them over.

- Napoleon's ruthless suppression of the hens demonstrates his willingness to use terror and murder to achieve his own ends, in the same way that Stalin executed and exiled those peasants who opposed him.

THE PIGS

- From the start of the story the pigs, in general, are seen as the most intelligent and capable creatures.

- As a group, they understand Animalism and translate it into easy slogans for the other animals.

- They quickly become the decision-makers on the farm. They become an elite class, exploiting the animals and living a life of luxury that is unimaginable to the rest of the farm animals.

THE CAT

- We hear very little of the cat once Napoleon is in power.

- She appears to represent the forces of self-interest and hypocrisy – as we see when she attempts to persuade the sparrows to read.

- She has as little as possible to do with the revolution, but is willing to enjoy its benefits.

GRADE BOOSTER

Think about how the sheep become unknowing tools of oppression. Each time a potential moment of protest comes up, their bleating prevents anyone else from being heard, and in this way they stifle any chances of free speech on the farm.

GRADE BOOSTER

Think about the dominance of the pigs from the start of the story. You could argue that their pre-eminence suggests that equality of any kind is unlikely, especially as the pigs are able to manipulate an ignorant crowd so easily.

By the end of the story, Mr Pilkington and the pigs are seen as allies – albeit temporarily. In the same way, Stalin and Churchill were allied at the Tehran Conference with Roosevelt. That this trust is only a façade is apparent in the allegations of cheating that close the story – as the Cold War reflected a rapid deterioration in the relationships between Russia and the Western powers after the Second World War.

MR PILKINGTON

- A farmer, like Mr Jones, Mr Pilkington in the allegory stands for Britain under Churchill.

- Like Napoleon, Mr Pilkington is keen to exploit his own workers. He is not a model farmer: Foxwood Farm is described as overgrown and neglected (p. 41), while its owner enjoys fishing and hunting. In this respect, he is presented as a gentleman farmer.

MR FREDERICK

- No more likeable than Mr Pilkington, Mr Frederick does at least run his farm a little better. He is a hard businessman and argumentative but shrewd (p. 41).

- His most striking characteristic is his cruelty.

- Napoleon's efforts to trade and bargain with Mr Frederick are a misguided attempt at business as Mr Frederick tricks him (p. 89). In a similar way, Hitler and Stalin's non-aggression pact was completely ignored by Hitler when he invaded Russia. This invasion was a violent and destructive one, in the same way as the attack on the windmill is seen as a demolition of all that the animals have achieved (p. 92).

MRS JONES

Very little is seen of Mrs Jones in the book but when she is mentioned it is in an unfavourable light – she is either snoring or running away from the farm.

DID YOU KNOW

The cartoon version of *Animal Farm*, made by Halas and Batchelor in 1954, was funded by America's CIA (Counter Intelligence Agency) as anti-communist propaganda – hence the 'happy ending'.

MR WHYMPER

The solicitor profits from the animals' misery and suffering – as the result of his dealings with Animal Farm he can buy himself a dogcart. He is described as 'a sly-looking little man' (p. 64). Even his name sounds pathetic.

EXAMINER'S TIP: WRITING ABOUT OTHER HUMANS

None of the humans in *Animal Farm* are seen as attractive, appealing or trustworthy characters. Even the minor characters are repugnant. The man who becomes Mollie's owner is described as 'a fat red-faced man in check breeches and gaiters' (p. 50) while the man who drives Boxer to his death is described as 'a sly-looking man in a low-crowned bowler hat' (p. 104). The repeated reference to the slyness of the human characters emphasises their unpleasantness and untrustworthiness. However horrifying the result of Napoleon's rule, Orwell seems to suggest that the animals were right to rebel against Jones's cruelty.

Progress and revision check

REVISION ACTIVITY

❶ How is Napoleon described? (Write your answers below)

....

❷ What do the animals think about Snowball just after the revolution and how do their feelings towards him change?

....

❸ Why does Mr Pilkington send Napoleon the message 'Serves you right'?

....

❹ What does Benjamin finally decide to read to the other animals?

....

❺ Whose skull has been buried by the end of the story?

....

REVISION ACTIVITY

Write down answers to these questions:

● Choose a character whom you liked or disliked and follow their part in the story.

Start: *A character I really liked (or disliked) was … and the part he/she played in the story was …*

● Look at the character of Clover. Is she an important character or not?

Start: *I think Clover is (is not) an important character because …*

GRADE BOOSTER

Answer this longer, practice question about the characters of the book:

Q: Examine the characters of Benjamin and Mollie in the story. Explore their different reactions to the revolution.

Think about:

● What happens to them in the story

● How they use their ability to read

● Their attitude to humans – and later the pigs

For a C grade: Convey your ideas clearly and appropriately (you could use the words from the question to guide your answer) and refer to details from the text (use specific examples).

For an A grade: Make sure you comment on the use Orwell makes of these characters, in particular the language used by Orwell and the animals' symbolic roles. If possible, come up with your own or alternative ideas.

Key contexts

THE AUTHOR

George Orwell was the pseudonym of Eric Arthur Blair, who was born in Bengal, India on 25 June 1903. Before the publication of *Animal Farm*, Orwell was better known as a journalist and social commentator than a novelist.

Orwell was a life-long socialist whose political beliefs led him to fight for the Republicans against Franco's fascists in the Spanish Civil War (1936–9). When the Second World War broke out, ill-health prevented him from signing up.

In 1947 Orwell moved to the Scottish Hebridean island of Jura. He died of tuberculosis in 1950.

PERSONAL EXPERIENCES

Orwell's experiences in the Spanish Civil War are relevant to the explicitly political *Animal Farm*. He became disillusioned with revolutionary politics after seeing the in-fighting between people who were meant to be on the same side.

Orwell wasn't just making a point about events in Russia in *Animal Farm*. He stated that the book was an attack on dictatorships in general and the way in which they seized and held on to power. He was not against revolutions but he did want to show people what happened when the people who led the revolution were allowed to do as they pleased.

SETTING AND PLACE

The book is set on a farm, an unlikely setting for a revolution. Orwell paints a fairly realistic depiction of farm life: the feeding, watering and milking of the animals are all described. The farm animals are anthropomorphic, although they still behave in ways characteristic of their species.

KARL MARX AND COMMUNISM

Marx believed that in a capitalist society workers were exploited by the people they worked for. Workers were paid a wage to produce goods that were then sold at a higher price than they cost to make. The difference between the cost price and the price the object is sold at is called profit. Marx argued that the capitalists kept this profit and that if they paid the workers lower wages, they could increase their profit. For this reason, the capitalists and the workers would never see eye-to-eye, or have each other's best interests at heart. According to Marx, this situation created a class struggle. Marx said that eventually the workers would rebel against the capitalists and overthrow them. They would then establish a more equal society.

Marx wrote *Das Kapital*, which stated that society should be free and equal, and the *Communist Manifesto*, which called for workers to unite. Lenin took Marx's ideas and adapted them to form his own brand of Communism.

AN ALLEGORY OF RUSSIAN HISTORY

Animal Farm is an **allegory** of Russian history. In 1917 the February Revolution overthrew the **Tsar**, but within months the Provisional Government was itself overthrown by the Communist Party, led by Lenin.

The struggle for power

Lenin died in 1924. A struggle for power between Trotsky and Stalin followed. Trotsky believed that to protect the Soviet Union, the revolution had to spread throughout the world in a 'Permanent Revolution', a slogan that encapsulated his beliefs. Unlike Trotsky, Stalin felt that the country's security lay in building its defences: 'Socialism in one Country' was his competing slogan.

The Soviet Union under Stalin

By 1928, Stalin had become a dictator. His rule seemed to have little in common with the ideas of either Lenin or Marx.

Propaganda was a frequently used tool that further emphasised the control Stalin had over Soviet life. Stalin frequently reinvented his history and that of the Soviet people. Past enemies were presented to the people as allies and vice versa. Those who were thought to oppose him were exiled or executed. In many cases 'show trials' were staged in which people confessed to crimes that they had not committed. These purges (the official name given to Stalin's elimination of his opponents) created a climate of fear.

Stalin exiled Trotsky in 1929. In Trotsky's absence, Stalin blamed him for the country's problems and claimed Trotsky was working with the country's enemies to overthrow the government.

? DID YOU KNOW

The Russian leader criticised in *Animal Farm* was born Joseph Djugashvili but later changed his name to Stalin, which means 'Man of Steel'.

REVISION ACTIVITY

Look at the following pages and the way in which Orwell changes the sequence of Russian historical events in *Animal Farm*. Make a note of exactly which events are altered.

- What effect do these changes have on the book?

- How does changing the order of the historical events on which the book is based help Orwell to get his political points across to the reader in *Animal Farm*?

Direct parallels

Certain real historical events correspond directly to events in *Animal Farm*, although the order of events does not exactly mirror Soviet history. The following are the main points of comparison:

Events in the Soviet Union	Events on Animal Farm
The Communist Party under the leadership of Lenin rose and took power, seizing control of the empire and executing the Romanovs (the Tsar's family).	Under the leadership of Major, the animals revolt against Jones and drive him from the farm.
Communism was strongly influenced by the idea that life could be explained in economic and social terms. It is based on the belief that the rich capitalist class exploited the proletariat and this situation could only be reversed by revolution.	Animalism is founded on Major's ideas in Chapter 1. These ideas echo many of Marx's theories.
After the Revolution, Trotsky and Lenin established a Communist society in the Soviet Union (as it was then called). All property, wealth and work was meant to be divided equally between all individuals.	The pigs attempt to create Major's ideal society and change the farm's name from Manor Farm to Animal Farm to reflect this new beginning.
Forces loyal to the Tsar, helped by countries abroad (who did not want Communism to spread throughout Europe), invaded Russia. Trotsky's brilliant command of the Red Army meant that the Bolsheviks stayed in power.	Jones and his men attempt to recapture the farm in the Battle of the Cowshed. Snowball's clever tactics mean that the animals win.
After Lenin's death, a struggle for power took place between Trotsky and Stalin. Trotsky, although favoured by Lenin, was beaten by Stalin who then tried to eliminate all trace of him. Trotsky was forced to leave the Soviet Union. He was sentenced to permanent exile in 1929.	Napoleon and Snowball disagree on virtually every issue. At a meeting in the barn, Napoleon drives Snowball from the farm. Napoleon and Squealer later tell the animals that Snowball is an enemy of Animalism. Napoleon claims Snowball's idea for the windmill as his own and Snowball's actions during the Battle of the Cowshed are completely distorted.
Stalin insisted that all farms should be collectivised (come under state control). These large collective farms had to give their produce to the government, which was opposed by the peasants. He also tried to modernise Soviet industry through his Five-Year Plans – the success of which he then exaggerated.	Napoleon instructs the hens to sell their eggs, but they smash them rather then let him sell them, in the same way that the peasants opposed collectivism. The animals work hard to build a windmill on the farm. Napoleon shows Whymper the apparently full grain stores (which are mainly filled with sand).
The Soviet Union endured several famines as the result of Stalin's economic policies. It is thought that 5 million people starved to death between 1932 and 1934.	The animals suffer increasingly from hunger after Napoleon comes to power, while the pigs are well fed.

Events in the Soviet Union	Events on Animal Farm
Stalin's power increased so that he had complete control over the Soviet Union. Stalin created a 'cult of personality' around him. Russians were told that he was the wisest man in the world. Pictures of him were displayed in schools and factories. He used propaganda to convince the Russian people that only he could protect them.	Napoleon uses a combination of terror and propaganda to become a dictator. Squealer is crucial in convincing the animals that Napoleon has only their best interests at heart. A portrait of Napoleon is painted on the barn wall. Songs, poems and speeches praising life on the farm are written.
Stalin used the murder of a potential rival, Kirov, in 1934 as an excuse to eliminate anyone who he thought was a threat to him. Between 1934 and 1938, 7 million people disappeared, many of them ordinary Russians. Most were executed or sent to gulags (slave labour camps). The most important victims were given 'show trials' and made to confess publicly to non-existent crimes, often to save their families from punishment.	Napoleon uses Snowball's alleged destruction of the windmill to get rid of the four porkers who protested against the abolition of the Sunday debates and the hens who led the egg rebellion. They confess publicly to ridiculous crimes before being slaughtered. Even Boxer, having defended himself against one of the dogs, is later eliminated – once he has served his purpose.
In an effort to protect the Soviet Union from attack, Stalin negotiated with both Britain and Hitler's Germany. His treaty with Germany was seen as worthless when Germany invaded the Soviet Union in 1941. The Germans were later defeated at the Battle of Stalingrad, but not before Russia suffered heavy casualties.	Napoleon has dealings with both Frederick and Pilkington over selling the timber and is finally tricked by Frederick who pays in forged notes. The animals defeat Frederick's men in the Battle of the Windmill but it is a hard and painful struggle.
At the Tehran Conference in 1943, the Soviet Union, Britain and the United States of America claimed to be allies. A few years later, the Cold War began, which placed the Soviet Union against its wartime allies.	The pigs and farmers have dinner together but their friendship is destroyed when both sides are discovered to have cheated at cards.

EXAMINER'S TIP: WRITING ABOUT CONTEXT

As the table above shows, the historical context for *Animal Farm* is very important. It is also fair to say that the book is Orwell's own creation, and that it is possible to write interestingly about it without making reference to the context. But understanding the history of the early twentieth century, and how Orwell responded to it, will enrich your answers and impress the examiner!

Key themes

POWER CORRUPTS

As well as an allegory of Russian history, *Animal Farm* can also be taken as a more general analysis of the search for power. It explores the ways in which corrupt figures can gain and manipulate power for their own purposes. *Animal Farm* exemplifies Lord Acton's famous words: 'power corrupts and absolute power corrupts absolutely'. As the pigs gain power, it becomes harder for them to resist the temptations of an easier life – especially as the other animals are too gullible to avoid being manipulated.

Major's speech presents us with a possible utopia: a perfect society, but we see that putting his ideals into practice is not easy. The animals' dependence on the pigs proves to be a fundamental stumbling block.

REVISION ACTIVITY

Here are some of the conditions on the farm that enable the pigs to gain power. Can you think of any more?

- Before Major's speech the pigs automatically assume a prominent position: '… then the pigs … settled down in the straw immediately in front of the platform.' (p. 13)

- The revolution is led by the pigs from the start. It is Major who inspires the revolution and the pigs who galvanise the other animals: 'The work of teaching and organizing the others fell naturally to the pigs, who were generally recognized as being the cleverest of the animals.' (p. 23)

- We are told several times that the pigs are the most intelligent animals on the farm 'Major's speech had given to the more intelligent animals on the farm a completely new outlook on life.' (p. 23)

HOW DO DICTATORS KEEP POWER?

Napoleon soon emerges as the farm's leader. His is a slow descent into tyranny. He is driven by power and throughout the book we see him plan to secure his hold on the farm and the other animals.

Dictators often rewrite history to produce a more flattering account of the past. Squealer completely misrepresents Snowball's actions during the Battle of the Cowshed and glorifies Napoleon's supposed bravery (p. 76). As readers we remember that Napoleon was absent from the battle – with the implication that this was a result of his cowardice. The animals have to depend on their own memories, which (as a result of Squealer's persuasive telling of partial truths) become less and less reliable.

EXAMINER'S TIP: WRITING ABOUT NAPOLEON'S POWER

By the end of the book, Napoleon's farm has become a totalitarian state. The animals have no control over any aspect of their lives and Napoleon's power over them is absolute. In this way, Orwell not only illustrates how Stalin came to power but also provides a textbook account of how dictators seize and keep power.

EDUCATION AND LEARNING

There is a proverbial saying that 'knowledge is power'. The pigs are clearly the most intelligent animals on the farm and soon take control of its management.

Initially they support the revolution by teaching its ideas to the other animals. As most of the farm animals cannot remember Major's speech and his ideas clearly, the pigs simplify them into seven slogans or Commandments. Snowball tries to teach the other animals to read and write.

Increasingly, however, the pigs take advantage of the other animals, instead of leading and helping them. The gulf between the ideals of the revolution (what the pigs pretend they are doing) and the reality of their actions becomes wider.

The role of education is an important one in the book. The pigs are able to dominate the animals as they can read; and, with the knowledge they acquire, are able to achieve and hold on to power. Snowball is able to prepare for Jones's attack as he has read a book of Caesar's campaigns (p. 43) and is full of ideas for 'innovations and improvements' for the farm (p. 50) that he has learnt from reading *Farmer and Stockbreeder*.

REVISION ACTIVITY

Through the characters of Snowball and Napoleon, Orwell presents two contrasting views of education.

- Snowball wants to educate all the animals but to some extent his attempts are doomed.

- Napoleon concentrates his efforts on a small group, with more success.

Can you find more examples of how the characters differ with regard to education?

LANGUAGE AND POWER

The pigs are able to exploit the other animals as they are intelligent enough to manipulate the truth so that their evil actions seem perfectly acceptable. This is achieved through their skilful use of language. The other animals have less control over language as is demonstrated by the difficulties they experience when learning to read. This means they are powerless in the new society and makes them vulnerable to exploitation by those animals who can use language cleverly – the pigs.

Orwell was very concerned about the relationship between language and power. His work at the BBC made him particularly aware of the ways in which language could be manipulated to change its meaning. In his essay 'Literature and Totalitarianism', Orwell stated that 'totalitarianism has abolished freedom of thought to an extent unheard of in any previous age'. He believed that this was achieved not only by preventing or forbidding certain thoughts or ideas but by telling people what to think. In this way, the totalitarian state doesn't just control your actions and movements but your thoughts as well.

GRADE BOOSTER

How would the revolution have been different if the other animals were able to read and write as well as the pigs? Go through the book and find points where you think the animals might have had a chance to question the pigs' actions. What prevents them from doing this?

KEY CONNECTION

In Orwell's novel *Nineteen Eighty-Four* we are told that Syme is working on a dictionary that removes words from the language. This reduces people's range of thought and their ability to protest.

PROPAGANDA

The pigs control the animals through their clever use of propaganda – a method of convincing others of the truth of your arguments. Squealer is the chief propagandist in the book and can 'turn black into white' (p. 23).

GRADE BOOSTER

Look carefully at the times when slogans are used in the story. Which animals use these slogans and how does their use of them differ? Explain the effect the slogans have on the other animals.

EXAMINER'S TIP: WRITING ABOUT THE USE OF SLOGANS AND JARGON

Snowball is the first to simplify language, when he reduces Major's ideas into the Seven Commandments of Animalism and then further into slogans such as 'Four legs good, two legs bad' (p. 37). Snowball also twists language by using vocabulary that the animals won't understand when he suggests that a wing should not be counted as a leg, as it is 'an organ of propulsion and not of manipulation' (p. 37). The use of jargon makes the speaker sound clever and the technique is used by Squealer to hide his real meanings and motives.

REVISION ACTIVITY

Here are some techniques that Squealer uses to convince the animals of Napoleon's wisdom and justice. Can you find any more examples?

- He reads out lists of statistics that have been forged.

- He tells them of written evidence (which he never produces) to prove that Snowball is in league with Jones, knowing that the animals cannot read.

- He makes selective use of the truth by telling the other animals that milk is good for the pigs (p. 38). It is, but it is also good for other animals on the farm, such as the hens.

- He uses rhetorical questions which do not require an answer from the audience – so the speaker does the thinking for them, 'Surely, comrades, you do not want Jones back?' (p. 56).

MEANING AND CONTROL

Language was important to Orwell who felt it was often used to manipulate the truth. He felt that sloppy language made it easier to present outrageous ideas in such a way that they seem acceptable. Orwell said that 'the slovenliness of our language makes it easier for us to have foolish thoughts.' In *Animal Farm*, we see several examples of this, from Squealer's use of the word 'readjustment' (p. 98) to tell the animals that their rations are being reduced, to the final perversion of the word 'equality'.

The slogan 'ALL ANIMALS ARE EQUAL BUT SOME ANIMALS ARE MORE EQUAL THAN OTHERS' (p. 114) is nonsense but its use disguises the inequality on the farm. The pigs have created their own version of the truth, changing Snowball's actions at the Battle of the Cowshed, and they themselves decide what language means. Words like 'equality' have their meanings deliberately altered to the extent that they actually lose their meaning.

Some people argue that this is not just a feature of totalitarian governments. Orwell's warnings about the ways in which words and their meanings can be twisted are still relevant today.

Progress and revision check

REVISION ACTIVITY

❶ What does Manor Farm represent at the start of the book? (Write your answers below)

....

❷ What does the destruction of the windmill signify?

....

❸ Why is the theme of education central to this book?

....

❹ Why did Orwell focus on propaganda in *Animal Farm*? How is propaganda used in the book?

....

❺ Why do the sheep only bleat slogans?

....

REVISION ACTIVITY

On a piece of paper write down answers to these questions:

● Would you consider the animals' ability (or inability) to read to be an important theme in the book?

Start: *I would consider the animals' ability (or inability) to read to be an important theme in the book because...*

● Think about the theme of power. Where does a character use physical force to gain power?

Start: *A character most obviously uses physical force to gain power when...*

GRADE BOOSTER

Answer this longer, practice question about a theme of the story:

Q: What techniques are used on Animal Farm to keep Napoleon in power?

Think about:
● The role of Squealer and his use of language
● The use of terror and an external threat to keep the animals in check
● The use of rumour and hearsay
● Napoleon's use of meetings, parades and ceremony

For a C grade: convey your ideas clearly and appropriately (you could use the words from the question to guide your answer) and refer to details from the text (use specific examples).

For an A grade: make sure you comment on Orwell's purpose in writing the story and what he wants us as readers to think about Napoleon. Consider how Orwell exploits the gap between what the animals think is happening and what we as readers can see Napoleon doing to gain and secure power.

Language

Here are some useful terms to know when studying *Animal Farm*, what they mean, and how they appear in the book.

Literary term	Means?	Example
Irony	When a writer uses words that suggest the opposite of what they normally mean.	The weekly 'Spontaneous Demonstration' on p. 100 is actually planned by Napoleon.
Satire	A written attack that makes something look foolish or unpleasant – ironic humour is often used to draw our attention to follies that the author is attacking.	Minimus's poem is unintentionally humorous as we can see the gap between his description of the farm and the reality of life under Napoleon.
Allegory	A story that mirrors historical events or wider ideas.	The Battle of the Cowshed mirrors the events of the Civil War in Russia.
Fable	A short story that contains a moral message.	*Animal Farm* is not simply a story about a farmyard – it teaches that power corrupts.

DID YOU KNOW

It is thought that Orwell's experience at the BBC may have provided the inspiration for 'Newspeak', in *Nineteen Eighty-Four*.

MANIPULATING LANGUAGE – AND PEOPLE

One of Orwell's main concerns was the way in which language could be used to manipulate and mislead people. This concern is reflected in *Animal Farm* and in his later work, *Nineteen Eighty-Four*, which features an official language, 'Newspeak', which is used by those in power to enforce particular ways of thinking.

LANGUAGE USED BY THE PIGS

The pigs – and in particular Squealer – manipulate language to control the farm. The techniques they use include:

- **Rhetorical questions:** The animals are repeatedly asked if they want Jones back: 'Do you know what would happen if we pigs failed in our duty? Jones would come back!' (p. 39).
- **Statistics:** Squealer tells the animals that they eat more and work less: the opposite of the truth. They create an illusion of life on the farm that the animals are incapable of questioning (p. 98).
- **Subversion:** The pigs completely change the meaning of words. They use the word 'equality' to mean its opposite. It is logically impossible for anyone to be 'more equal' than another.
- **Simplification:** Major's maxim 'Whatever goes upon two legs, is an enemy. Whatever goes upon four legs, or has wings, is a friend.' (p. 18) is reduced to the slogan 'Four legs good, two legs bad' (p. 37). The less intelligent animals adopt this reductive phrase, which becomes a way of silencing dissent.

- **Obfuscation**: The pigs deliberately mislead the animals by using words that they find confusing: 'Squealer always spoke of it as a "readjustment, never as a reduction"' (p. 98).
- **Distortion:** The meanings of words are twisted out of shape, reducing language to nonsense: 'A too rigid equality in rations … would have been contrary to the principles of Animalism' (p. 97).

SATIRE

Animal Farm is a satire on political power. Orwell achieves this in the following ways:

- **Animal stereotypes:** His choice of animal to represent different historical figures or ideas is satirical. He uses mainly negative representations, e.g. the sheep (traditionally regarded as stupid animals) are used to represent the public as an unthinking 'mob' and a donkey (an animal we tend to think of as stubborn) is the farm's cynic, Benjamin. The satire is effective as Orwell expects us to be aware of how the characters should behave, e.g. Major's speech sets out a standard of correct behaviour which, as the story unfolds, the pigs ignore.
- **Political allegory:** The symbols used are obvious – as you would expect in an allegory. The farm represents Russia; Napoleon represents Stalin. The satire also makes complex political events, like the German invasion of Russia (the Battle of the Windmill), easy for us to understand.

STYLE

Orwell's style is so 'transparent' and simple that it is hard to realise that our views of the story's events and characters are being carefully directed. He manipulates our reaction to the book in a number of ways:

Fairytale phrasing

- **Simple language:** The book contains the sort of language we would expect to find in a fairytale. Phrases like 'As soon as the light in the bedroom went out there was a stirring and a fluttering all through the farm buildings' (p. 13) encourage us to think that this will be a traditional children's story. Animals are introduced to us in a list-like way as they come into the barn. The narrator acts as a traditional storyteller, using phrases such as 'Now, as it turned out' (p. 25) to give us a sense of a story unfolding before us.

Getting the point across

- **Economy:** Orwell uses an economical, spare paragraph structure to emphasise particular points: 'It was a pig walking on his hind legs.' (p. 112)
- **Repetition:** Some simple phrases are repeated. We are often told that the weather is harsh and that the animals 'worked like slaves' (p. 61) or are hungry. Orwell uses these key phrases to remind us throughout the book of the animals' suffering and the real result of the pigs' actions.
- **Descriptive language:** There is little figurative language used in *Animal Farm*. Orwell's language becomes more descriptive when the animals look at their farm during the harvest after the revolution and after the execution (Chapters 2 and 7). Even so, the writing here is still strictly controlled and simple; in Chapter 2, for example, the animals kick up 'clods of the black earth and snuffed its rich scent' (p. 27).

EXAMINER'S TIP

When you write about the language used in *Animal Farm*, you must provide a quote to support your answer and explain *why* Orwell uses it.

IRONY

Irony is the use of words to express something different from, and often opposite to, the literal meaning. There are many examples of irony in *Animal Farm*.

[Exploiting the farm animals]

- We are told that the animals have 'hardships' to face but that they also have 'a greater dignity' in their lives than before as there are 'more songs, more speeches, more processions' (p. 99–100). The reader can see that these are simply ways in which the pigs control the animals.

- The animals' pride that their work is 'for the benefit of themselves' and not for 'idle, thieving human beings' (p. 61) is undercut by the reader's awareness that the animals are being exploited in exactly this way by the pigs.

[Ridiculing Napoleon]

- By reducing well-known political figures to the level of farmyard animals (and unflattering ones at that), Orwell trivialises and ridicules his targets, e.g. Napoleon's black cockerel and the poems composed in his honour (p. 100) are seen as ludicrous, contrary to the effect of grandeur and power for which Napoleon strives.

COMEDY AND THE PIGS

Comedy is also used by Orwell for satirical effect. When the pigs get drunk in Chapter 8, their behaviour is amusing. The fact that the pigs think Napoleon is dying, when it is clear to us that he has a hangover, is funny – we don't expect animals to behave like that. However, we are also told repeatedly at the start of the book that Jones drinks heavily and that this is one reason that he neglects the farm. The pigs' behaviour in Chapter 8, then, is not just comic, but also shows the way in which the pigs come to resemble Jones in his greed and lack of concern for the animals' welfare.

EXAMINER'S TIP

When you write about language, bear in mind Orwell's purpose in writing *Animal Farm*. He wanted to make a specific political point and so uses a range of techniques to drive his point home to us. Think about how the language at the beginning of Chapter 1 before the revolution and at the close of the book shows us how life on the farm has come full circle.

DESCRIPTIVE LANGUAGE AND THE REVOLUTION

Orwell uses descriptive language in order to leave us in no doubt that the revolution is a good thing. The description of the farm after the revolution is poetic ('sweet summer grass') and contains an evocative physical description of the animals' activities ('snuffled its rich scent') (p. 27).

The detailed description of the farm in Chapter 7 and the emphasis on its natural beauty is used to create an image of what the animals have lost and how the revolution could have turned out. Orwell contrasts two different visions: the ideal of the freedom and peace that the animals could have achieved is set against the terrifying reality of their lives (and the terror of the farmhouse after Jones has left). The reader is reminded of what the revolution was meant to do and how these ideals have been betrayed.

Structure

As befits an allegory, the sequence of events in *Animal Farm* mirrors those of the Russian Revolution and its history under Stalin. The novel is divided into ten chapters, and the farm's decline into tyranny is marked by the gradual violation of each of the Seven Commandments.

In Chapter 2, the new dawn on p. 27 is symbolic as well as literal. It is as though the animals have woken from a sleep. Chapter 2 makes us aware of just what the animals have fought for and how happy they are with the equal society that they think they have created after the revolution.

The book charts the corruption of Major's ideal in stages: Chapter 1 sets out the rebellion's high ideals and acts as a marker by which we judge the pigs' subsequent actions.

The turning point comes once Napoleon orders the execution of the pigs and the hens. Then there is a speedy descent into further betrayal – Boxer's death and tyranny. Life deteriorates quickly once life has been taken – and it is not long before the pigs are walking on their hind legs, installing a phone and dressing in human clothing (p. 114).

By end of book, Napoleon sleeps in Jones's bed, dines from his crockery and drinks alcohol. The circular nature of the plot is used by Orwell to highlight the depth of Napoleon's descent and the irony of the revolution. He is worse than Jones as he has betrayed the animals' trust.

SUBTITLE AND STRUCTURE

Animal Farm is still popular because of its apparent simplicity. The book is set in a farmyard, its storyline progresses in clear stages, its main characters are animals: it seems at first to be a perfect children's book. The simplicity of the book supports its subtitle 'A Fairy Story'. The simple storyline; straightforward, sometimes comic, characters and seemingly naïve tone stop *Animal Farm* from being seen as a dry political pamphlet and allow Orwell's message to reach the widest possible audience in a readable form. Even so, the book was rejected by publishers numerous times because of its anti-Stalinist message.

Orwell does, however, subvert the genre he is writing in. We expect fairytales to be about the battle between good and evil – as in *Animal Farm* – but in this book, good is seen to be punished rather than rewarded. The ending's ambiguity leaves the reader thinking the worst – that there is no possible happy ending to the story. We don't expect fairytales to be nightmares. *Animal Farm* is not really a fairy story at all, but a bleak political satire.

DID YOU KNOW

Although *Animal Farm* was written in 1943, it was seen as too politically sensitive to publish and was rejected by several publishers (incuding the poet T. S. Eliot). It wasn't until 1945 that it was finally printed by Secker and Warburg.

GRADE BOOSTER

Consider how the events in the farmhouse at the end of Chapter 10 would come across if they were seen from Napoleon's or Benjamin's point of view. What effect would losing an omnipotent view of events have on our under-standing of this final scene?

NARRATOR

Orwell uses a third person narrator to tell us the story of Animal Farm. A third person narrator is a god-like, omnipotent figure, who sees everything that happens in the story – and can even tell us what each character is thinking.

Most fairy stories and fables have a third person narrator, but there are also other reasons why Orwell uses this technique:

- **Detachment:** Orwell's narrator seems detached and gives the reader a similar distance from events in the book. Although we are often given the animals' interpretation of events, Orwell is careful to use phrases that leave us in no doubt about what is happening. For example, when Squealer is found at the bottom of the ladder in the middle of the night, it is described as 'a strange incident which hardly anyone was able to understand' (p. 94). The animals might not be aware of what is going on but it is obvious to us that Squealer has been caught red-handed changing the Commandments, and has fallen off the ladder as he is drunk. The gap between what is really happening and what we are told is exploited by Orwell to make a satirical point.

- **Trust:** We trust the narrator. We do not question his interpretation of the characters and we believe that he is telling the truth and showing us all that happens on the farm. This relationship between reader and narrator is problematic and perhaps ironic in a book that is itself about the way in which language can be distorted.

A SHIFT IN TONE

In the final scene in the book there is a shift away from Orwell's detached narrator to the tone of a dream or vision. This shift is emphasized by Orwell's repetition of the animals' trust in the pigs and that the promised utopia will arrive some day (p. 111–12), followed by Clover seeing the pigs walking on their hind legs, and the acceleration towards the final scene. The contrast highlights the extent of the pigs' betrayal and exploitation of the animals.

FABLE

The story has similarities to another genre – the beast fable – in which animal characters are used to make serious moral points. In these works, such as *Aesop's Fables*, the characters do not behave in a realistic way but are symbolic of certain attitudes. Animals are often the main characters in children's books (such as *The Wind in the Willows* or *The Jungle Book*) for a similar reason. They do not have to be as 'realistic' as characters in other books and can be given one single, overriding personality trait.

Unlike most beast fables, though, the ending of *Animal Farm* is ambiguous. There is no clear sense of how life will turn out for the animals. No clear moral is stated, although Orwell's message throughout the text is clear.

Progress and revision check

REVISION ACTIVITY

❶ What is satire? Give an example of satire in the story. (Write your answers below)

....

❷ How does the animals' use of the word 'comrade' change over the course of the book?

....

❸ Why are phrases such as 'the animals worked like slaves' repeated so often?

....

❹ How does the farm setting help Orwell determine the structure of the book?

....

❺ Contrast the Battle of the Cowshed with the Battle of the Windmill.

....

REVISION ACTIVITY

Write down answers to these questions:

● Find two examples of irony in *Animal Farm*.

Start: *One example of irony in Animal Farm is …*

● Find examples where the story's narrative viewpoint changes and explain the effect this has on the reader.

Start: *An example of when the narrative viewpoint changes is when…*

GRADE BOOSTER

Answer this longer, practice question about the structure of the story:

Q: To what extent is *Animal Farm* a satire?

Think about:
● Orwell's use of allegory
● Characterisation
● Irony
● The book's subtitle

For a C grade: convey your ideas clearly and appropriately (you could use the words from the question to guide your answer) and refer to details from the text (use specific examples).

For an A grade: make sure you show that you understand Orwell's purpose in writing the story and how the structure and use of character, language and form drive this home to the reader. These points need to be woven into your answer.

PART SIX: GRADE BOOSTER

Understanding the question

Questions in exams or controlled conditions often need **'decoding'**. Decoding the question helps to ensure that your answer will be relevant.

 ## UNDERSTAND EXAM LANGUAGE

Get used to exam and essay style language by looking at specimen questions and the words they use. For example:

Exam speak	Means?	Example
'convey ideas'	'get across a point to the reader': usually you have to say how this is done	Napoleon's pomposity is conveyed when he appoints a black cockerel to act as his trumpeter (p. 100).
'methods, techniques, ways'	The 'things' the writer does: for example, a powerful description, introducing a shocking event, how someone speaks	Clover's shock is reinforced by Orwell's use of a one line paragraph to tell us what she has seen: 'It was a pig walking on his hind legs' (p. 112).
'present, represent'	1) present: 'the way things are told to us' 2) represent: 'what those things might mean underneath'	We are presented with the news that Squealer is 'unaccountably' absent from the Battle of the Windmill (p. 92). His absence at a key moment in the farm's history suggests cowardice, and represents hypocrisy, as Orwell's ironic language implies.

 ## 'BREAK DOWN' THE QUESTION

Pick out the **key words** or phrases. For example:

Question: How does Napoleon rise to power? How does Orwell **portray** Napoleon at the **start** of the book and at its **end**?

- **Portray** – how does Orwell show us what Napoleon is like?
- **Start** – how does Napoleon behave just after the rebellion?
- **End** – what has Napoleon become by the end of the book?

What does this tell you?

- **Focus on:** Orwell's description of Napoleon at the start of the book; the Seven Commandments as a structural device; Squealer and his use of language; Napoleon's use of terror; Boxer's death; Napoleon's resemblance to Mr Jones.

 ## KNOW YOUR LITERARY LANGUAGE!

When studying texts you will come across words such as 'theme', 'symbol' and 'imagery'. Some of these words could come up in the question you are asked. Make sure you know what they mean before you use them.

Planning your answer

It is vital that you **plan** your **response to the controlled assessment task or possible exam question** carefully, and that you then follow your plan, if you are to gain the higher grades.

 DO THE RESEARCH!

When revising for the exam or planning your response to the controlled assessment, collect **evidence** (for example, quotations) that will support what you have to say. For example, if preparing to answer a question on why Orwell uses a farm as the book's setting, you might list your ideas as follows:

Key point	Evidence/quotation	Page
The farm provides a clear allegorical framework for the story. At the start of the book, it is rundown and poorly managed, mirroring Orwell's view of Russian life under the Tsar.	'the hedges were neglected, and the animals were underfed.'	p. 25

 PLAN FOR PARAGRAPHS

Use paragraphs to plan your answer. For example:

❶ The first paragraph should **introduce** the **argument** you wish to make.

❷ Then, **develop** this argument with further paragraphs. Include **details**, **examples** and other possible **points of view**. Each paragraph is likely to deal with one point at a time.

❸ **Sum up** your argument in the last paragraph.

For example, for the following task:

Question: Discuss the significance of the Seven Commandments in *Animal Farm*, and how Orwell uses them to develop key themes within the book.

Simple plan:

● Paragraph 1: *Introduction*, e.g. Explain book's allegorical nature

● Paragraph 2: *First point*, e.g. Association with Christianity's Ten Commandments

● Paragraph 3: *Second point*, e.g. Established for all animals to understand the revolution's principles

● Paragraph 4: *Third point*, e.g. Gradual distortion of rules by Napoleon and Squealer's justifications for this

● Paragraph 5: *Fourth point*, e.g. Use of the Commandments by Orwell to show Napoleon's transition to dictatorship

● Paragraph 6: *Conclusion*, e.g. Sum up their value to Orwell as a structural device

How to use quotations

One of the secrets of success in writing essays is to use quotations **effectively**. There are five basic principles:

❶ Put quotation marks, e.g. ' ', around the quotation.

❷ Write the quotation exactly as it appears in the original.

❸ Do not use a quotation that repeats what you have just written.

❹ Use the quotation so that it fits into your sentence, or if it is longer, indent it as a separate paragraph.

❺ Only quote what is most useful.

 USE QUOTATIONS TO DEVELOP YOUR ARGUMENT

Quotations should be used to develop the line of thought in your essays. Your comment should not duplicate what is in your quotation. For example:

GRADE D/E   GRADE C

(simply repeats the idea)	(makes a point and supports it with a relevant quotation)
When Napoleon gives the signal, there is the sound of the dogs barking outside the barn, 'there was a terrible baying sound outside' (p. 54).	When Napoleon gives the signal, terror is heightened through the description of the 'terrible baying sound outside' (p. 54).

However, the most sophisticated way of using the writer's words is to embed them into your sentence, and further develop the point:

GRADE A

(makes point, embeds quote and develops idea)
The 'terrible baying sound outside' (p. 54) heightens the terror of Snowball's expulsion from the farm and also emphasizes the animals' confusion at what unfolds in front of them, building the tension before the dogs actually appear in the barn.

When you use quotations in this way, you are demonstrating the ability to use text as evidence to support your ideas – not simply including words from the original to prove you have read it.

EXAMINER'S TIP

Try to use a quotation to begin your response to a question. You can use it as a springboard for your own ideas, or as an idea you are going to argue against.

Sitting the examination

Examination papers are carefully designed to give you the opportunity to do your best. Follow these handy hints for exam success:

 BEFORE YOU START

- Make sure that you **know the texts** you are writing about so that you are properly prepared and equipped.

- You need to be **comfortable** and **free from distractions**. Inform the invigilator if anything is off-putting, e.g. a shaky desk.

- **Read** the instructions, or rubric, on the front of the examination paper. You should know by now what you need to do but **check** to reassure yourself.

- Before beginning your answer have a **skim** through the **whole paper** to make sure you don't miss anything **important**.

- Observe the **time allocation** – and follow it carefully. If the paper recommends 45 minutes for a particular question on a text make sure this is how long you spend.

 WRITING YOUR RESPONSES

A typical 45-minute examination essay is between 550 and 800 words long.

Ideally, spend a minimum of 5 minutes planning your answer before you begin.

Use the questions to structure your response. Here is an example:

Question: Look at how Orwell presents the relationship between Napoleon and Snowball. How does it alter as the story progresses?

- The introduction could briefly describe **who** the characters are and **what they represent**.

- The second part could describe how Orwell presents their relationship at the **start of the book**.

- The third part could explain what other characters say and think about them by the **end of the book**.

- The conclusion would **sum up your own viewpoint**.

For each part, allocate paragraphs to cover the points you wish to make (see **Planning your answer**).

Keep your writing clear and easy to read, using paragraphs and link words to show the structure of your answer.

Spend a couple of minutes afterwards quickly checking for obvious errors.

GRADE BOOSTER

When writing about characters it is important to describe *why* Orwell makes them behave in certain ways.

 'KEY WORDS' ARE THE KEY!

Keep on using the **key words** from the question in your answer. This will keep you on track and remind the examiner that you are answering the question set.

Sitting the controlled assessment

It may be the case that you are responding to *Animal Farm* in a controlled assessment situation. Follow these useful tips for success.

 KNOW WHAT YOU ARE REQUIRED TO DO

Make sure you are clear about:

● The **specific text** and **task** you are preparing (is it just *Animal Farm*, or more than one text?)

● How **long** you have during the assessment period (i.e. 3–4 hours?)

● How **much** you are expected or allowed to write (i.e. 1,200 words?)

● **What** you are **allowed to take** into the controlled assessment, and what you can use (or not, as the case may be!). You may be able to take in brief notes but not draft answers, so check with your teacher.

 KNOW HOW YOU CAN PREPARE

Once you know your task, topic and text/s you can:

● Make **notes** and **prepare** the points, evidence, quotations, etc. you are likely to use.

● Practise or draft **model answers**.

● Use these **York Notes** to hone your **skills**, e.g. use of quotations, how to plan an answer and focus on what makes a top grade.

★ **GRADE BOOSTER**

When writing about Orwell's use of language you should explain the effect that it has upon the reader.

 DURING THE CONTROLLED ASSESSMENT

Remember:

● **Stick** to the **topic** and task you have been given.

● The allocated **time** is for **writing**, so make the most of it. It is **double** the time you might have in an exam, so you will be writing almost **twice as much** (or more).

● At the end of the controlled assessment follow your teacher's **instructions**. For example, make sure you have written your name **clearly** on all the pages you hand in.

Improve your grade

It is useful to know the type of responses examiners are looking for when they award different grades. The following broad guidance should help you to improve your grade when responding to the task you are set!

GRADE C

What you need to show	What this means
Sustained response to task and text	You write enough! You don't run out of ideas after two paragraphs.
Effective use of **details** to **support** your **explanations**	You generally support what you say with evidence, e.g. When the ducklings enter and Clover makes 'a sort of wall round them with her great foreleg' (p. 14), we see that she is kind, protective and maternal, a sympathetic character.
Explanation of the writer's **use of language**, **structure, form**, etc., and the **effect on readers**	You write about the writer's use of these things. It's not enough simply to give a viewpoint. So, you might comment on how contrasts are used. You might compare the description of the pigs in the farmhouse (p. 114) with the descriptions we are given of Mr Jones earlier in the book.
Appropriate comment on **characters, plot, themes, ideas** and **settings**	What you say is relevant and is easy for the examiner to follow. If the task asks you to comment on how Snowball is presented, that is who you should write about.

GRADE A

What you need to show *in addition* to the above	What this means
Insightful, exploratory response to the text	You look beyond the obvious. You might question whether the revolution would have succeeded under Snowball and the wider points Orwell makes about power and democracy.
Close analysis and use of **detail**	If you are looking at Orwell's use of language, you carefully select and comment on each word in a line or phrase, drawing out its distinctive effect on the reader, e.g. when mentioning the new horses as 'willing workers and good comrades but very stupid' (p. 109), Orwell makes the point that it is in the pigs' interest for Boxer's replacements to be even less intelligent than him.
Convincing and **imaginative interpretation**	Your viewpoint is likely to convince the examiner. You show you have **engaged** with the text, and come up with your own ideas. These may be based on what you have discussed in class or read about, but you have made your own decisions.

Annotated sample answers

This section provides you with **extracts** from two **model answers**, one at **C grade** and one at **A grade**, to give you an idea of what is required to achieve at different levels.

Question: To what extent is Boxer a significant character in *Animal Farm*?

CANDIDATE 1

Boxer is an important character in *Animal Farm* and a character Orwell wants us to like. We first see him when he walks into the barn. He is described using a simple simile which is he is 'as strong as any two ordinary horses put together' and friends with Clover but not very clever. 'He was not of first rate intelligence.' Other animals respect him because he works hard and is strong. This tells us what Orwell meant. He is selfless too – when Snowball tells the animals not to wear ribbons, Boxer throws away his hat.

Because *Animal Farm* is an allegory, Orwell uses characters like Boxer to make us think about people's lives in Russia and wants us to care about them. Perhaps Boxer represents ordinary people who don't question what's going on. Boxer sits carefully down in the barn 'lest there should be some small animal concealed in the straw', which shows he cares about other people and is gentle, even though he is big.

Orwell shows us Boxer's gentleness again when he is upset because he thinks he has killed the stable lad. 'I had no intention of doing that.' Even when Snowball tells him that it is good to have killed him, Boxer says he didn't want to and begins to cry.

Another point to show Boxer is important is that he is responsible for getting in the harvest and building the windmill. The farm wouldn't work without Boxer. 'Boxer was the admiration of everybody.' This shows he is significant on the farm and this adds to the story and what happens later because it makes it tragic when all his hard work is ruined.

Orwell's methods are by getting us to like Boxer we think he is a good, strong horse and don't like the way he is treated by the pigs – this creates sympathy when we read which is important, too.

Boxer is killed because he didn't understand what was happening and trusted the pigs. His motto is 'Napoleon is always right.' This means the pigs can use him to do exactly what they want with him. They even buy a crate of whisky with the money they get for selling him to the knacker and this sums up the whole tragedy of what happens to him.

Gives other characters' opinion of the character

Quote doesn't quite match the point made

Interesting but not developed enough

Good understanding of text and character

Good use of quotation

Quotation not embedded into the sentence

Too vague a statement – this needs to be explained in detail

Some awareness of the writer's purpose and use of character

Correctly focuses on passage to make a point which is then supported and reinforced

Need to provide example of language used

Overall comment: A solid essay with a good grasp of the text. Points are generally supported with evidence but are not developed fully. Reflects a sound knowledge of the character and awareness of authorial purpose but points need to be better structured, focus more on how effects are achieved and could be linked more fluently.

GRADE C

CANDIDATE 2

Clear, fluent opening states Boxer's symbolic role and how he engages with the reader

Boxer, the considerate, loyal workhorse (who represents the working classes on whom the success of the revolution was built) is one of the most sympathetic characters in *Animal Farm*, and therefore significant in terms of how the reader is drawn into the text. Orwell's choice of an 'enormous' horse, capable of doing the work of 'two ordinary horses', emphasises and symbolises the sheer power of the Russian working class. He is the 'admiration of everybody', as he works tirelessly to support the farm, and throughout his significance as a worker and selfless comrade is stressed.

Orwell also wants us to admire Boxer's noble nature: he is a gentle giant, as we see when he tries to avoid crushing 'some small animal concealed in the straw'. This gentleness provides a contrast to the pigs' ruthlessness – early in the book, when he laments that he had 'no intention' of killing the stable lad, Snowball criticises Boxer for his 'sentimentality'.

This section amplifies the previous point and uses interpolated quotation to good effect

As the story continues, we become aware of the injustice and exploitation that the horse suffers under Napoleon, culminating in his death. Orwell uses Boxer's death as a symbol which highlights how corrupt Napoleon becomes. Earlier Major had told Boxer that Mr Jones would sell him to the knacker. The significance here is that the pigs do exactly the same and that doesn't make them as bad as the humans, but in fact worse as we see how much Boxer trusted the pigs. Napoleon betrays Boxer, just as he betrays Major's ideals.

Boxer's death is the emotional climax of the book, once again an important moment both narratively and in terms of how we as readers respond. Boxer doesn't know what is happening to him and the pathos of his fate reinforces its injustice.

Good use of literary term but the points are unsupported by textual evidence

In conclusion, Boxer is a highly-significant character because he symbolises the common people through whose eyes we see the new regime and believe it will herald a golden age and through whose eyes we see the corruption and deterioration of that ideal.

Clear sense of author's purpose supported with evidence.

Use of mature vocabulary

A good detached awareness of the text but no supporting quotation

Overall comment: An excellent structured response with a few weak points. The main areas of Boxer's story and his role in the book are discussed fully, with quotations and evidence woven skilfully into the answer, complete with references to Orwell's use of language. The student demonstrates some original thinking and ideas. However, there is a tendency to miss supporting evidence in places.

GRADE A

Further questions

❶ What is a satire? With reference to *Animal Farm*, identify the targets that Orwell attacks. Is he successful?

Write about:
- the events that happen in the book
- the use of language and structure.

❷ Look at the relationship between Napoleon and Snowball. How does it alter as the story progresses?

Write about:
- the methods Orwell chooses to present their relationship
- what others think and say about these characters.

❸ How are the changing actions of the pigs used to show the breakdown of the Seven Commandments?

Write about:
- the original reason for the Seven Commandments
- how the lives of the animals change.

❹ How different do you think the farm would have been under Snowball?

Write about:
- what Snowball does and what happens to him
- what Orwell tells us about the other animals.

❺ What do you learn about the role of Boxer in the book?

Write about:
- Boxer's strengths and weaknesses
- how Napoleon and the other pigs treat Boxer
- how Orwell uses Boxer to raise ideas.

❻ Orwell uses a simple story to express complex ideas. What do you think he is trying to show us in his presentation of the pigs and how they treat the other animals, over the course of the book?

Write about:
- Orwell's use of fable and what we usually expect to find in a fable or fairy story
- how the pigs' behaviour contrasts with the ideals set out in Major's speech.

❼ In what ways is Squealer an important character in the novel?

Write about:
- his use of language in the book
- the methods Orwell uses to present him to the reader.

❽ How are certain words or phrases altered in *Animal Farm*? Who changes them?

Write about:
- the Seven Commandments
- what we learn of Orwell's ideas about language.

❾ *Animal Farm* is subtitled 'A Fairy Story'. How suitable is this description of the book?

Write about:
- what we expect to read in a fairy story
- Orwell's use of irony.

❿ How important is the issue of education in *Animal Farm*?

Write about:
- Napoleon and Snowball's differing attitudes to education
- how the animals try to read and write.

Literary and political terms

Literary term	Explanation
allegory	a story with two different meanings, where the straightforward meaning on the surface is used to reveal a deeper meaning underneath
anthropomorphic	a description of animals that are seen to behave like humans. They talk and think, for example
beast fable	a fable that makes use of anthropomorphic characters
character(s)	either a person in a play, novel, etc. or his or her personality
fable	a short story that contains a moral
figurative language	any form of language that contains more than the bare facts and is used to create effect, e.g. her head was spinning
genre	a type of literature, for instance poetry, drama, biography, fiction; or style of literature, for example, gothic or romantic
imagery	descriptive language which uses images to make actions, objects and characters more vivid in the reader's mind. Metaphors and similes are examples of imagery
irony	when someone deliberately says one thing when they mean another, usually in a humorous or sarcastic way
jargon	language that has a pretentious vocabulary or meaning, often linked to particular subjects or professions
maxim	a short and effective statement which suggests ideal ways of behaving
narrator	the voice telling the story or relating a sequence of events
obfuscation	the deliberate use of words to mislead an audience
propaganda	the deliberate and organised spread of information to make sure that people unquestioningly believe what you want them to believe. It is also used to refer to the information itself. Propaganda is not in itself good or bad – it depends on the purposes to which it is put and on who the audience is and what it believes
proverb	a short saying that deals with a generally accepted truth, for example, 'Too many cooks spoil the broth'
pseudonym	a name that a person uses instead of their real name
rhetoric	the art of speaking (and writing) effectively so as to persuade an audience
rhetorical question	a question that does not require an answer but is used to emphasise a particular point
satire	literature that targets an issue, institution or idea and attacks it in such a way as to make it look ridiculous or worthy of contempt. It is not the same as simply making fun of something, as the satirical writer has a purpose in attacking the target, other than making people laugh
symbolism	using an object, a person or a thing to represent another thing
theme	a central idea examined by an author
third person narrative	a story that is told by an unseen narrator who does not use 'I', but uses 'he', 'she' and 'they'
utopia	an imagined perfect place or society

Political term	Explanation
Bolsheviks	the radical wing of the Marxist Russian Social Democratic Party. Founded by Lenin, the Bolsheviks came to power in the 1917 October Revolution and eventually changed their name to the Communist Party of the Soviet Union
capitalist	according to Karl Marx, a capitalist is someone who has money and invests it in a business. This person then makes a profit if the business does well
Cold War	the period from 1949 to 1989, which was marked by a diplomatic and political standoff between the Soviet Union and Western powers
democracy	a government that is elected by the people or their representatives
dictator	a ruler whose decisions do not need anyone else's agreement. Often, in dictatorships, any form of opposition has been abolished, leaving the ruler with absolute power
indoctrination	brainwashing someone into believing a particular opinion
kulak	a land-owning peasant. After the Russian Revolution, the kulaks did not want their farms to be collectivised. From 1929, Stalin began to exterminate them as a class
marxist	a follower of the ideas of Karl Marx (1818–83)
proletariat	the lower or working class, especially those living in industrial societies whose only possession (according to Marx) was the value of their work
republic	a form of government where the people – or the people they elect – have power
subversive	description of someone or something that is working to destroy something, particularly a government (often behind the scenes/in secret)
totalitarian	description of a government that has absolute control over its citizens' lives and does not allow them to raise any opposition. Most dictatorships are totalitarian
Tsar	the emperor of Russia until 1914. The word is also used to mean a tyrant, or autocrat, or – more generally – a person in authority
tyrant	a person who governs in an unjust and violent way. Someone who uses their power in an unreasonable or selective way to oppress others can be said to be tyrannical

Checkpoint answers

Checkpoint 1
The animals' names often suit their personalities and draw attention to a particular characteristic. Napoleon was a French emperor who was widely regarded as a tyrant; this is an effective and economical way of getting information across to a reader. For more examples, see the **Characters** section.

Checkpoint 2
The way that Jones mistreats the animals makes us feel sympathetic towards them. Orwell also spends some time introducing the animals. We get to know their characters and start to care about them. Then, when Major tells us how badly mankind treats the animals, we feel sympathetic towards them.

Checkpoint 3
Snowball and Napoleon are introduced as 'Pre-eminent among the pigs' (p. 23) and so we are alerted to their importance in the book. Look at the individual descriptions that follow and how they hint about future events.

Checkpoint 4
The fact that the animals remain speechless when they walk through the farmhouse is not seen as sinister in Chapter 2. However, later in the book, the animals' inability to express their thoughts and opinions is one reason why the pigs are able to exploit them further. Look at which animals are able to articulate their feelings and whether or not they do so.

Checkpoint 5
The animals' reading abilities – and their attitudes to education – vary considerably and reinforce certain stereotypes about them. Look at what the different animals choose to read too (pp. 36–7): for example, the dogs read only the Commandments, showing their fanatical support for the pigs' regime.

Checkpoint 6
Squealer's use of the word 'duty' suggests that the pigs are responsible for the wellbeing of the other animals on the farm. Squealer presents the pigs' greed as an act of self-sacrifice to the other animals. The pigs' grip on power tightens in this chapter.

Checkpoint 7
The use of the word 'order' tells us that the pigs are now making decisions without consulting the other animals. The idea of equality on Animal Farm is being abandoned – you do not order your equal to do something, you ask them! Not only are the pigs taking control, but they are also using their power for selfish reasons.

Checkpoint 8
Orwell shows us how unpleasant the humans in *Animal Farm* are so that, even after Napoleon has taken power, we do not think that the solution to the animals' problems is to return to life under Mr Jones or another human. The fact that life on Animal Farm is worse than on the farms run by humans shows just how corrupt and cruel Napoleon has become.

Checkpoint 9
Mollie's love of sugar – as well as her love of ribbons – shows us that she is only interested in her own wellbeing. The sugar is given to her by the humans and shows her willing enslavement to them. Mollie isn't interested in the politics of the farm around her – only in superficial rewards.

Checkpoint 10

Napoleon spends his time between meetings 'canvassing support' (p. 50) from the other animals and uses the sheep's bleating to silence his opponents. Napoleon, we are told, 'seemed to be biding his time' (p. 51) and Napoleon's planning is evident when we see the puppies emerging as savage guard dogs.

Checkpoint 11

With clever language, Squealer convinces the animals that Snowball is a criminal and says that Napoleon is protecting them from their own stupidity and the threat of Mr Jones's return. The animals are made to feel guilty for questioning Napoleon and are frightened by the possibility that Mr Jones might come back. The dogs' presence also intimidates them into accepting what they are told.

Checkpoint 12

Squealer asks the animals if they can produce any written evidence of a resolution against trade. The animals, of course, cannot and even if they could, it is doubtful that they would be able to understand it. Squealer uses the animals' ignorance against them.

Checkpoint 13

When the four pigs confess to colluding with Snowball, we are told that 'the dogs promptly tore their throats out' (p. 78). Eventually there is a 'pile of corpses' and 'the smell of blood'. Orwell describes the executions in a calm and detached way that emphasises their horror.

Checkpoint 14

The animals are confused and 'shaken' (p. 78) by the savagery and speed of the killings but they believe that the dead animals were guilty. They are unable to express what they feel and think. The only way they can protest at what has happened is by singing 'Beasts of England' – which is immediately banned.

Checkpoint 15

Napoleon does not deserve his medals, as his cowardly actions at the Battle of the Cowshed show. The fact that he awards them to himself shows that they have no merit and are simply there to make him appear brave and add to his prestige as the leader of Animal Farm.

Checkpoint 16

The pigs now wear green ribbons to show that they belong to an elite. Mollie was told by Snowball that ribbons were 'the badge of slavery' (p. 24) – they are now marks of distinction. This reminds us that the pigs have turned the original ideas of the revolution upside down.

Checkpoint 17

There is only one candidate for leadership of Animal Farm: Napoleon. The election is not a free or democratic one: it is clearly rigged. The claim that the farm is a republic is false. The animals have no say in how the farm is run.

Checkpoint 18

The pigs behave like parasites – there are more of them and they do very little work. They live very comfortably in the farmhouse and eat well while the others starve. Napoleon is being hypocritical.